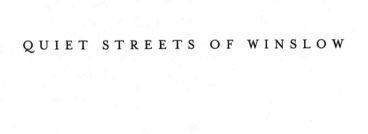

QUIET STREETS OF WINSLOW

QUIET STREETS OF WINSLOW

A Novel

JUDY TROY

COUNTERPOINT
BERKELEY

Library of Congress Cataloging-in-Publication Data

Troy, Judy, 1951-
The Quiet Streets of Winslow : a novel / Judy Troy.
ISBN 978-1-61902-239-3
1. Murder--Investigation--Fiction. 2. Arizona--Fiction. 3. Mystery fiction. I. Title.

PS3570.R68Q54 2014
813'.54--dc23

2013026168

ISBN 978-1-61902-239-3

Cover design by Charles Brock, Faceout Studios
Interior design by meganjonesdesign.com

COUNTERPOINT
1919 Fifth Street
Berkeley, CA 94710
www.counterpointpress.com

Printed in the United States of America
Distributed by Publishers Group West

10 9 8 7 6 5 4 3 2 1

To Georges and Anne Borchardt
And Miller

"There is a crack in everything. It's how the light gets in."

— LEONARD COHEN

chapter one

TRAVIS ASPENALL

Y BROTHER AND I were walking Pete in the wash of the Agua Fria when he caught a scent and we found her. This was before school, in the windy dawn. Her eyes were wide open, brown eyes staring straight up at the pale sky.

"We better close them, Travis," Damien said, and I nodded, but we knew better than to touch her. Her arms and legs were flung out as if somebody had tossed her down into the wash, as if she wasn't wanted anymore.

She was maybe four or five inches shorter than I was, thin and small, like even her bones were small. She was wearing a gray sweater and jeans and cowboy boots, and the boots reminded me of our mother's, with stenciling up the sides. But she was much younger than our mother was. She had short, dark hair and pale skin, pale enough to make her look like a tourist, only she didn't look like a tourist. She had a bracelet on her left wrist with a cross dangling from it, which made me wonder if she had been Catholic, like we were, and was somebody we had seen at church. I thought she looked a little familiar.

There were bruises on her neck, and her head didn't lay right, which was how I guessed that her neck was broken, that maybe somebody had broken it with their hands. The April wind was blowing down from the mountains and for half a second I thought she might be cold and almost took off my jacket to cover her.

Pete was nosing at her clothes. He was part Rottweiler and part some kind of hound, our father said. Our dad was a veterinarian—not here in Black Canyon City, but in Cave Creek, twenty miles down the interstate and a few miles to the east. Somebody had brought Pete into Dad's clinic and said, "I can't keep him anymore. You may as well put him to sleep," and Dad brought him home instead. The dog's name had been Butch, but Damien had called him Pete from the start, so we kept it.

"Get away from the body," I told him, and he stepped away and sniffed at a tumbleweed. We had had Pete's sister and brother, also, until they had died last year, but Pete had always been the most intelligent.

My brother Damien couldn't stop looking. Even when we had started home, he kept looking back as if he couldn't believe in that dead body being there. He was ten and I was fourteen. We didn't look alike. He had blondish-brown hair and green eyes, like our mother, and would probably be tall, someday, like her side of the family, whereas I was dark and on the small side, like Dad. Damien was a better athlete than I was. I liked fooling with a basketball in the parking lot of the Mission Church, where Father Sofie had put up a hoop, but the only thing I could do well was dribble. I felt that nobody could steal the ball away from me, but people could and did. For some reason that always surprised me.

I was walking fast and Damien walked fast to keep up with me. We lived on Canyon Road, north of the Agua Fria. You turned onto the gravel drive just past the cattle guard, and our stucco house was fifty yards or so farther in. It had been my mother's idea to paint it blue. My father had built the house small, believing that people needed just so much, that anything more would cause you grief somehow. Nobody lived close to us. It was just desert all around, with saguaros and cholla and mesquite and creosote and the wind blowing all the time. If you climbed the desert ridge behind our house, you would be looking in the direction of the Perry Mesa National Monument, which tourists got lost every year looking for.

Parked next to our house was the Airstream we had lived in while our house was being built. Our half brother, Nate, stayed in it when he came to visit, and we all thought of it as his now. When he visited he almost never got up as early as we did, unless he happened to have been awake all night. Then you'd see him sitting on the steps of the Airstream in the morning, just sitting by himself as if he thought something might happen.

From a distance I could see my mother on the patio, looking for us; we'd been gone so long. When we told her she got Dad out of the shower and he called Deputy Sheriff Sam Rush, and when Sam arrived he told Damien and me to keep this to ourselves. Not to say a word to anybody. Then Sam and Dad headed to the wash. They had known each other since high school. Sam was six three and weighed some seventy pounds more than Dad. They were mismatched friends, my mother liked to say.

"You two sit down and eat," Mom said to Damien and me. "Focus on school today. You have that history test, Travis. Whatever happened to that dead woman has nothing to do with you."

Mom was wearing jeans and a blue shirt and her long hair was wet from the shower. She spoke sometimes about cutting it, and Dad would protest. I liked long hair as well, although the girl I liked happened to have short hair, like the woman in the wash.

Pete's water bowl was empty, and when I started to get up to fill it Mom said, "You don't have time for that," and did it herself. Then she opened the kitchen door and stood in the doorway, shading her eyes from the blaze of sun appearing.

"Finish eating and get your backpacks," she said to us. "Your buses will be here soon."

Damien and I would be on Trail Road by the time Dad and Sam Rush returned, and we wouldn't learn until later that the dead woman was Jody Farnell, whom we had seen once when we were visiting our half brother, Nate, in Chino Valley. Nate had taken us to a Denny's for breakfast and she had waited on us and Nate had said to Dad, "Leave her a good tip. She has a kid."

Later, in science class, I would wonder whether you would be able to hook a brain up to a computer, one day, so that you could download what a murdered person had seen and heard and thought before she died. I imagined that it would be there, in the brain cells, the way that DNA survived in a strand of hair. Then I would think about Harmony Cecil—the girl I liked—and wish there was a way to get inside her head, to make her think about me more often than she did, or to change the thoughts she might already be having.

Anyway that was how it started—with that April morning Damien and I took Pete for a walk before school.

chapter two

NATE ASPENALL

I USED TO FOLLOW Ernest Sterling around, back when he and my mother, Sandra, were together and I was in middle school. Ernest was a handyman, basically, a hippie handyman who smoked pot on his way to this or that job, and I'd go with him, Saturdays, to watch him unclog a drain or replace a washer, insulate a ceiling or install a swamp cooler.

"Watch how I do this, Nate," he would say, and I'd be there at his elbow, handing him a wrench or a Phillips. He was muscular and tattooed, with hair to his shoulders and a moustache dripping down either side of his mouth. Being stoned never seemed to get in his way. In his truck, those mornings, I would say, "Let me have a toke. It's not like I haven't gotten high before," and finally he would let me, and it was like I was watching myself in a movie, all morning, watching myself act the role of a thirteen-year-old kid following this father figure around. At home, for lunch, Sandra put a frozen, family-size Mexican dinner in the microwave, and I ate almost all of it myself, and Sandra said to Ernest, "I can't fucking believe you would do this," and she got his clothes out of her bedroom closet and threw them on the front porch.

I tell this story to show that nobody knows what's best for another person.

YEARS LATER, I used the skills I had learned from Ernest to get my job at the Chino Valley RV Park, earning a small salary and bartering a place to live in exchange for keeping the narrow gravel roads smooth and the RVs in running order, and some years after that was when I met Jody Farnell. She was waitressing at the Denny's on Mirage Highway, where I ate breakfast, and from the moment I saw her, before I had heard her voice, even, I felt a physical shock, as if I had just taken off in a rocket or woken up from a coma. I'm not sure I ever stopped feeling that. In that flesh-pink uniform with her pale skin and brown eyes she looked so young you wouldn't have guessed that she had a child or that she had lived the complicated life I was to find out about.

I was thirty-two to her twenty-three, and five mornings a week with her bringing me coffee and pancakes I learned that she had come to Chino Valley with a boyfriend she wasn't with anymore, and that she was renting a motel room by the month. I also learned that her daughter, Hannah, lived with Hannah's father, only nobody knew where, and that Jody wanted to get Hannah back from him. With some people you could see where the darkness was, and you knew better than to shine a light there, but she volunteered details: she and the father had hardly known each other; she had been struggling with drugs, back then, which was why Hannah's father had taken Hannah from her. He had been raised by a Navajo family near Winslow, Jody said, which was where Jody was from, too. The Navajo family hadn't wanted Jody to have Hannah either, even after Jody got clean. It seemed as if everybody had been against her.

I told Jody she could count on me if she ever needed anything—
seriously count on me, I said—and on a rainy October morning after
her motel room had been broken into she asked if she could stay with
me a few nights. She knew from Mike Early, who had the RV behind
mine, that the RV park was safe. She knew Mike Early from Denny's,
which he frequented quite a lot.

"You can stay with me as long as you need to," I told her, and she
brought over her belongings and slept in the built-in bed in my RV,
while I slept on the futon couch in what was essentially the living room.
She talked about looking for a place of her own, but I said, "You don't
have to," and after a week she dropped the subject and I was relieved.

Jody was tiny. Five feet one with bones so thin it made you ache to
look at her wrists. She fit into the RV alongside me, because I'm not a
big person either. I'm small, for a man, five seven and 138 pounds no
matter how much I eat or how many weights I lift. I take after Lee, my
father, more than I take after Sandra. I have dark hair and eyes, like
Lee and my half brother, Travis, whereas Sandra is blonde and blue-
eyed. The Honda dealership she worked for used her face on billboards,
but up close she was tenser and older looking than you would have
expected. She and Lee had been seventeen when they had me, and I used
to try and guess how many times they had thought *no way* before they
gave in and let me come.

I never introduced Sandra and Jody to each other. I didn't like the
thought of them forming ideas about each other, or ideas about me
based on what they thought of each other. I didn't want all that imagining going on. Moreover, I didn't want to jinx my situation with Jody. I
felt lucky to have found her, and luck was something you had to protect,
I had learned. It wasn't as if it came often or easily, at least not to me.

chapter three

SAM RUSH

I SHOULDN'T HAVE BEEN working the case, given how long I had
known Nate Aspenall and how close I was to the family, but there
was just Kurt Hargrove and myself deputy-sheriffing the more than eight
thousand square miles that made up Yavapai County, and Kurt would
have had to take the time to get to know the family and the situation.
Moreover, I thought it likely that Kurt, or anyone in Kurt's position,
might not have looked as carefully elsewhere once he had Nate as a
suspect. Nate did not have a criminal history, but he was a solitary,
underemployed, thirty-two-year-old male who had known the victim,
and the victim's body had been found near his father's house, 150 miles
from where the victim was living. I knew what I would have thought; I
knew how it looked even to me. For my part, I had to be conscious of my
bias. I wasn't convinced I had one, which made me fairly certain I did,
and I knew it was crucial that I keep aware of it.

The details of the case were as follows: Jody Farnell had left Chino
Valley at the beginning of February, close to three months before she
was killed, and moved back to Winslow, where she had grown up. She
moved into a small rental on the corner of Hicks and Maple, across

town from where her mother was located, and when she wasn't able to find a job locally she looked for work in Flagstaff and was hired as a maid at a Hilton Inn.

The elderly woman living next door to Jody didn't often see her, but she had seen a man at Jody's front door two or three times, quite late. A medium-size male in his thirties, was her impression, with light hair; had she seen the same man mowing a yard down the street? It was possible. She never saw a vehicle. She would see him at Jody's door, then she would see him leaving on foot. She assumed Jody wasn't home or didn't feel like letting him in.

Jody's landlord, Paul Bowman, had been out of state with his wife at the time of the murder; I wasn't able to interview him at first.

Jody's mother I spoke to at the trailer she rented on the eastern edge of town. She was anorexically thin, from drug use, I surmised, and described herself as disabled. She chain-smoked while we talked. She said that Jody was supposed to have taken her to the pain clinic in Winslow the following day, which was how she knew that something was wrong. But she couldn't tell me anything about Jody's recent life. "Jody didn't confide in me," the mother said. "I don't know why we weren't close in that way." If Jody had had a boyfriend in Winslow, the mother didn't know about it, and while the mother had heard Jody mention the name Nate, she couldn't recall the context. About her granddaughter, Hannah, she knew little to nothing. She had not seen her since she was an infant. "That Indian family," she said, "who knows what they did to her? The baby's father stole her away." Jody's mother didn't know where they were.

As FOR THE death, itself, Jody's neck had been broken, probably by hand, by somebody who was left-handed, as Nate Aspenall was. There were no discernible fingerprints. There was some bruising on her upper arms, as if she had been either shoved or grabbed first. She hadn't been thrown down into the wash but positioned to look as if she had; there were no signs of her body having hit the rocks. Whether she had been killed there or brought there dead was hard to know. Footprints were hard to make out in the desert. I suspected she had been killed first, then carried there. She had not been raped, nor had she had intercourse within the previous twenty-four hours, but there were traces of semen in her mouth and on her chin. She had been dead for about ten hours by the time Travis and Damien Aspenall found her. Nine PM, then, she was killed, or close to it.

As I said, the fact that Nate Aspenall had known Jody, and that Jody had been found not in or near Winslow, where she was living, but near the Aspenalls, in Black Canyon City, made Nate a person of interest, despite the illogicalness of his having done something that pointed the finger at himself. He claimed to have been in Chino Valley the night of her murder, working on the RV behind his, trying to locate a water leak. He had worked until midnight, he said. The occupant of that RV was a sixty-two-year-old man named Mike Early, who worked at a Sears in Paradise Valley. I left messages and waited to hear back. Meanwhile, I spoke to the manager of the RV park, who said that he had no knowledge of Early's water leak but that Mike Early and Nate Aspenall were neighbors, and they were friendly with each other. Early had probably asked Nate for help directly. That often happened, the manager said. Often he—the manager—wouldn't learn until later what work Nate had done, when, and for whom.

I hoped that Nate living in an RV park, as opposed to the kind of isolated places where so many residents of Yavapai County lived, would make it easier for me to learn whether anyone else might have seen him at home the night of Jody's murder.

MY FIRST INTERVIEW with Nate took place on the telephone the evening of the day the Aspenall boys found the body. I talked to him from home, from my duplex on Abbott Street, across town from Lee and Julie's residence. Fifteen years earlier, Lee had lived in the left side of the duplex and I in the right; since then, I had bought and renovated both sides into a house for myself, and that was where I had lived since—other than my two years of marriage, when, at her request, I had moved into my wife's house.

"Tell me again, Nate," I said, "when you saw Jody last." I was at my kitchen table, next to the sliding glass door, with my small notebook in front of me.

"The last week in February," he said. "Maybe earlier. I'm not sure. I don't keep track of time. She asked me to meet her in Flagstaff, and I did and we talked. We met at a diner near the hotel where she worked, and she told me about her life in Winslow and the problems she was having."

"With what or with whom?" I said.

"She was afraid of somebody," Nate said. "She said a man was showing up late at her house, wanting to make a sexual arrangement with her, calling her all the time, looking in her windows. One night she was at a place called Bojo's, she said, having supper, and was almost sure she saw him hiding in the back hall, staring at her. She didn't know who he was, she said, and she didn't want to go to the police. She felt they would blame it on her, somehow. She didn't trust them."

"Had this man threatened her?"

"It sounded like it. Or else she felt threatened. She also said that her landlord had come on to her. He would charge her less rent, she said, or no rent, if she . . . well, you can imagine."

"She spelled out the sexual act he referred to?" I said.

"Yes."

"Was she asking you to do something about either of these men?"

"Not that I could see."

"So why do you think she wanted to tell you?" I said. "And why in person?"

"I've thought about that," Nate said. "I have. I think she wanted to see me worried about her—to see that worry in my face."

"Why?"

"She felt that nobody cared about her." He said that reluctantly, it seemed to me, as if he were revealing a confidence.

"Before this meeting," I said, "how often had you and Jody talked on the telephone?"

"Four or five times a week at first, then not as often. I would call her, and if she felt like it, she would call me back. She didn't always want to talk to me."

"Why was that?"

"Honestly?" he said. "My feelings for her were stronger than she wanted them to be. We weren't . . . when she was staying with me, we were roommates. That was how she was with me."

"So she wanted you to worry about her but she didn't want you," I said. "Is that what you're saying? That's a tough position to be in."

"Well, I was never popular with girls. You know that. I mean, I wanted to be, but I wasn't. I was used to that."

"Used to it or not, it would make most men angry."

"I'm not most men."

"What about after you saw Jody in Flagstaff?" I said. "How often did the two of you talk then?"

"Less so," he said.

"Why was that, do you think?"

"My guess is that she found some other man to worry about her."

"You mean, she found the person who ended up killing her?" I said.

"I don't know. Maybe."

I heard the sound of him walking around, pacing.

"Jody was wearing a bracelet with a cross on it," I said. "Did she go to Mass? Could she have met somebody at church?"

"Her dad gave it to her. That was what she told me. And no. She didn't go. She had this idea that God watched everybody all the time as a kind of hobby and decided who to remember and who to forget."

"So she believed in God but didn't trust him? Or what?"

"It was hard to tell."

"Did it matter to you, you and Jody both being Catholic? Did it make you feel closer to her?"

"I wouldn't have cared what religion she was."

"Do you go to Mass at all, Nate? I'm just curious."

"Sometimes when I stay with Lee and Julie. Julie asks me to, so I go with her and the boys."

"I don't know much about Catholicism," I said, "but I've always been interested in the idea of confession. You know why? Because in my world it doesn't happen often. Almost everybody says 'I didn't do it,' or 'I wasn't there,' or 'I have no idea what you're talking about.' Most of the time people say all three."

I laughed a little and Nate didn't.

"So you probably never believe anybody about anything," he said.

"I believe evidence," I said. "In that respect, my job is less complicated than most people think it is."

Nate was silent. I could picture the watchful, waiting expression on his face, which I had seen so often.

chapter four

NATE ASPENALL

FIVE THIRTY IN the morning I'd hear footsteps on the linoleum, then water running in the bathroom. Bath closet, Jody called it; she liked to name things. In the dim light of the kitchen I would see her in her nightgown, which was white flannel with a line of roses across the top. She would have makeup traces under her eyes and a flush to her skin that went away after she had coffee. Her lips were fuller after sleep, and she was unnaturally quiet in her movements, like she was there but she wasn't there, awake but still dreaming.

She made coffee and when it was done she poured herself a cup, stirred in cream and sugar, and took it back to bed with her. This was ritual—the same things in the same order every morning. She would sit up with a pillow behind her back and write in this flowered journal she had.

I think about you every morning and every night. I think about how small you were when I saw you last, and how much you must miss me. I'm your mother. You and I are part of each other.

Usually she carried that journal in her purse, but toward the end of her stay with me she got careless and I came across it. On the first page she had written: *You will soon have everything in the world that you desire.* Who would believe that? She had probably found it in a fortune cookie. She believed what she read and heard, as long as it was positive. If it wasn't, she told herself it couldn't be true, and I could never figure out if that was hope on her part, or ignorance. You should get a journal, she told me, but never said why, never explained what it did for her or what it would do for me. Maybe hers helped her believe what she wanted to.

It was dark, that early, with a moon, if there was a moon, and if the wind was blowing cold enough, she would turn on the electric heater and I would hear the hum of it. I would get coffee for myself and sit with a blanket over my shoulders, and when Jody was done writing she would make us breakfast. I never asked her to. I never asked her to help in any way. She did it on her own—scrambled eggs and toast—and I would clean up afterward while she was out walking, walking fast up and down the narrow roads of the RV park as if her thoughts were after her. With her small build you would think from far away that she wasn't done growing.

After her walk she often stopped at Mike Early's RV, behind mine, and had coffee with him before he went to work, and that was all right with me. He didn't have much going for him, and he was a good deal older. As I've explained, they knew each other from her waiting on him at Denny's. They were friends, and I liked him well enough myself. Mike was due to retire soon from the Sears in Paradise Valley, where he sold appliances. He and I used to eat together. He would grill hamburgers and tell me about his ex-wife, who wouldn't have divorced him if he hadn't drunk so much, smoked so much, eaten so much fried food, or slipped off to the casinos in Laughlin—if he had been perfect, in other words. He would smile but you could see that he was up nights, regretting it all.

After his wife divorced him, their son disappeared in the Grand Canyon. The son had been close to my age. He had lived with his mother, worked at a Cellular One, and had trouble keeping friends. He was taking a week off to hike in the Grand Canyon, he had told his father. He was seen hiking down into it and he never came out. Mike Early believed that one day his son would be found alive, although he knew better, and so did everybody he told it to.

That was a bond between Jody and Mike, the daughter who had been taken from Jody and Mike's son who had gone off and lost himself. That was what they talked about, Jody said, and sometimes they didn't talk at all, she said, but just sat together with their coffees and listened to the birds waking up outside. She said that nobody but a parent could understand.

I know you will come back to me, Hannah. Every person on earth and maybe in the universe has made a mistake, and you will, too, one day, and then you will see that people deserve to be forgiven.

Jody never wrote about me in her journal, even though I let her stay with me all those months. What that told me was what I should have known from the beginning—you can't wish or force yourself into somebody's heart. Up until I found her journal I believed I had a chance, and after I found it I guess I couldn't give up; it's hard to when what you want so much is so close. Could you make somebody want to do what they didn't want to do? It seemed there had to be a way, something you could say that would convince them, or soften them. Some side of yourself you could show them, which they had overlooked and could like you for.

Anyway, she lived with me from October through January. I think that was where I started. Every morning before dawn I saw her in her nightgown, floating in my kitchen.

chapter five

TRAVIS ASPENALL

"I T'S NOT AS clear as it could be, Lee," Sam Rush said to my father. "That's all I'm saying. I've spoken to some people in the RV park and there's now some question about it. I told Nate it would be helpful to the investigation if he could come stay here a while. I need more access to him."

I had taken Pete outside before Sam arrived, and when I heard Sam and Dad talking on the patio, I waited in the darkness behind the house before going in. By the time Sam left, my parents were sitting in the kitchen. The room was darkened; only the light over the stove was turned on. When my mother saw me she looked startled. She had forgotten I'd taken the dog out as she had asked me to.

"We're just talking," my father said. "All right? Make sure you get your homework done."

I walked past the den where Damien was watching *Star Wars* with the sound turned down low. He was supposed to be doing his math problems and had his book open in front of him on the rug. But he had forgotten about the book. That was how much he could get into a movie, even one he had seen twenty times before. I was different.

I went into the room he and I shared and looked over the poems I was supposed to read for English. I had tried to read them on the bus, but in the seat in front of me Nelson Rogers, who was two years ahead of me, was talking quietly to my friend Billy Clay about having had sex with Selena Maynard.

"Call her a few times, tell her you like her, and she might do it," Nelson said. "It doesn't take much."

Billy and I and our friend Jason Whitlow—the three of us had been friends since the second grade—had known Selena a long time. Billy had felt her up once at a party. That was what they used to call it, he said, when his dad was in high school. His dad had told him that when he was in high school, feeling a girl up was all most poor sods would get in high school. "Don't try for much more," his dad had told him. "It'll spoil you. You'll have nothing to look forward to after graduation."

Through the open window I heard my mother's wind chimes, then rain began, which didn't usually happen in April. It fell slowly at first, but before long it was steady and I gave up reading and listened to it, thinking about what Sam had said to Dad outside, knowing that it must have been about Nate's alibi. Then I thought about the fact that Nate had been on the wrestling team for a year in high school, as had I, in middle school, and that the first thing they taught you was how not to strangle somebody or break somebody's neck, how not to accidentally kill your opponent, which had happened at our high school once, fifteen years or so before I was born.

I countered it with thoughts of Nate taking Damien and me to Frontier Stables to go horseback riding, which he used to do when we were younger, or to Taco Bell, after school, or to the public pool in the summer. I thought about the time our parents were out and Damien

had an asthma attack. Nate had gotten us into his truck and driven fast
to Urgent Care. There were a lot of examples.

But Nate could be moody, and he used to have this habit of going
around in a raincoat in all but the hottest weather. Sometimes in public
you would see people reacting strangely to him, such as moving a few
feet away, in stores, and I'd move away so that nobody would know we
were related. Around Damien and me, Nate acted like a brother, but I
didn't know what he was like when he wasn't with us.

Damien came in and changed into pajamas. He said, "Dad said
Nate's coming tomorrow or the day after or something." Then he
closed his eyes and fell asleep within a few minutes. I didn't sleep as
well as he did. I would lie awake, thinking. Lately I would lie there trying to imagine what Harmony Cecil looked like without clothes on. In
addition to seeing her at school I saw her once a week at church. Like
me, she was Catholic, but not. She had given up on God last year, when
her brother lost an arm and a leg in Afghanistan. She had told me that
one Sunday after Mass. Her parents made her attend, and she sat in
the pew with them, but she no longer went to confession or received
Communion. I had never seen her brother. He didn't come home now
that he was disabled. He hadn't let them visit him when he was recover-
ing. The last time she had seen him was before he left for Afghanistan.

Through the window I could smell creosote in the desert and hear
the rumble of traffic on I-17, which was always in the background, far
enough away that it didn't bother you, but you would have noticed if it
wasn't there. I fell asleep and dreamed that Jody Farnell was trying to
tell me things about myself that only she knew. But I woke before she
could say the words. "The dead know our secrets," Harmony Cecil had
said the week before in English class. Did Mr. Drake know what story

or poem that might have come from? Harmony's grandmother said it every time they drove past a cemetery. But Mr. Drake hadn't known.

Harmony was one-fourth Navajo. A lot of people claimed to have Indian heritage, but you could see it in her black hair and round face. When she wore a white shirt it shone against her dark eyes and skin. I had had girlfriends before, girls I would be with for three or four weeks, but Harmony was the first girl I felt respect for. It wasn't automatic with her—liking you back just because you liked her. She had her own feelings she was loyal to. But she wasn't actually my girlfriend yet. For the last few weeks I had talked to her only at her locker and waited with her after school for her bus, which came before mine did. I had ridden my bike past her house plenty of times, but she didn't know about that.

The bedroom was cool, with the windows open, and the wind spun Damien's planetary mobile, which hung in the corner. Stars were light-years away, Damien had been learning at school. "If you could fly fast enough," he would tell us, "you wouldn't get older." He was always wanting to go backward. When he outgrew his clothes he wouldn't let my mother give them away, and he had the kind of nightmares younger kids had—monsters in the closet, snakes under the bed. "Hypersensitivity," my mother said. That was what the doctor had told her. Maybe it was hereditary; maybe Damien would outgrow it. All it meant was that Damien felt too much. "Quit taking him to church," my father told her. "That alone would make him less afraid."

I heard my parents' footsteps in the hallway, and after a few minutes I heard them talking. The walls in our house were thin. Sometimes I heard more than I wanted to. I would think, Fine, do it. That's how Damien and I got here. But don't make me listen to it.

"What time will he get here?" my mother said.

"He'll get here when he gets here. You know how he is. "

"Maybe we don't know him as well as we think we do," my mother said.

"I know Nate," my father said. "I know my children."

I fell asleep and woke later to the kitchen door closing. From the window I saw my father standing on the patio, smoking a cigarette. He had trouble sleeping, too, and as far as I knew that was the only time he smoked. But then there were things you would never know about your parents and things they would never know about you. There was always a way in which people in general were sort of strangers to each other.

chapter six

SAM RUSH

N ATE ASPENALL ARRIVED in Black Canyon City seven hours
later than he said he would. Six thirty the following morning Lee
got him up and the two of us walked him out to the wash and showed
him where the body had been found. Nate squatted down and touched
the rocks with both hands. His straight brown hair was thin, a bit strag-
gly. He had on loose-fitting jeans and a gray-and-black-checked flannel
shirt, worn almost threadbare. He had gotten a tattoo since I had seen
him last—Jody's initials, *JPF*, vertically on the back of his neck. Beside
the *J* was a small blue heart. He asked me when the funeral was going
to be and I told him that the mother wanted it to be private and he
expressed the view that that was selfish.

After we walked back I sat alone with Nate on the patio under
the corrugated roof, just off the kitchen where the wind wasn't strong.
There was a wicker table between us, and we both had gotten ourselves
coffee. Nate seemed formal with me. I was in uniform, and the fact
that he had known me all his life seemed to take second place to the
uniform. Perhaps he saw me as two people now and was trying to figure out how to talk to both of us at once. He was intelligent; he always

had been. Not great in school growing up, but quick and smart. He had done better in college, but had dropped out a few months before graduation.

"Let's go back to the night Jody died," I said. "It was Mike Early's RV that had the water leak, you told me. Where was the water leaking from?"

"A broken pipe under the shower," Nate said.

"He contacted you directly? Or spoke to the manager of the RV park and had the manager contact you?"

"Directly. We're friends. Friends the way that neighbors are."

Nate picked up his coffee.

"I've been to Chino Valley," I said, "and I've spoken to Mike Early. You and he both seem pretty certain what night that was, but the woman in the RV across from his said that Early wasn't home that night. She was sure of it. She said he hadn't been there all day, and that she didn't see him or his vehicle again until the following night. She didn't know whether or not you were home. She can't see your RV as easily."

"If you're talking about Doris Farmer," Nate said, "she'll say anything to anybody. Plus, you know how the RV park is laid out, with the trees. It's not all that easy to see what's going on."

"Unless you're nosy and make a point of it."

Nate glanced in the direction of the Airstream, which was thirty feet or so from where we sat. The sun had come up and was glinting off the silver.

"Well, it's possible I was wrong about what night Mike had that leak," he said. "Maybe he and I were both wrong. I get calls to fix things all the time. It's hard to keep track of what happened when."

He looked at his coffee, in which the cream was separating, and he put his index finger in and stirred.

"What kind of relationship did Jody have with Mike Early, from your perspective, Nate?"

"They were friends. I told you that. Mike was lonely, and his son had disappeared, which gave him and Jody a connection to each other."

"So Jody liked older men," I said.

"You mean, in general? No. I don't think so. But she did like Mike Early. We both did."

"Here's why I'm asking," I said. "Mike has a picture of Jody that was taken in his RV. She's sitting at his table in a plaid robe. His plaid robe. I asked him."

"You mean she's wearing it over her clothes."

"No," I said. "In place of."

Nate's eyes were down. He was sitting perfectly still.

"What did Mike tell you about it?" he said.

"That it was raining the day that picture was taken. That she had gone for a walk and gotten wet and stopped in for coffee, and that he had given her his robe to wear while he took her clothes to the laundry room you all share, up near the manager's office."

"Okay then," Nate said. "There was a good reason for the robe."

"Why wouldn't she have gone to your RV first to change out of her wet clothes?"

"Jody wasn't logical."

"Why do you think Mike would have that picture right out there," I said, "where anybody could see it?"

"Well, she's not naked or anything. So why shouldn't he have it out?"

"Maybe he likes the implication of the picture," I said. "And maybe he has reason to feel that way. Maybe the rain that day gave Jody an excuse to undress in his RV, to excite him, to entice him a little."

"I don't think she would have done that with him."

"So it's the kind of thing she might have done with somebody, but not with him?" I said. "What makes you so sure?"

Nate shook his head.

"I knew her and you didn't," he said.

"You could say that makes me the more objective one."

"Objective, maybe," Nate said, "but about somebody you never met, never talked to, never spent time with."

"Well, you're right about that," I said. "And so far you knew her better than anyone I've spoken to, which is why it's useful to me to have you here. It would be a help if you could stick around. Your dad said he would pay the rent on your RV until you were able to get back to Chino Valley."

"He told me."

"So just stay close, if you would," I said.

"For how long?"

"I don't know. Two or three weeks, maybe longer. We'll have to see. Can you do that?"

"Do I have to?"

"I was hoping you'd want to help."

The expression in his dark eyes was troubled, nervous, both resistant and compliant. He hesitated too long before answering.

"I'll stay as long as I can," he said.

chapter seven

NATE ASPENALL

I COULD ALMOST SEE her lying there, that was the eerie part. Like a dead bird with its wings spread out, or a deer lying still and whole on the side of the road. Lee didn't walk down into the wash with me, but Sam did, shadowing me with his large frame and big, plain face, and I put my hands on the ground, feeling the rocks and gritty sand, hoping I could feel something of her, her soul or spirit or whatever it was that didn't want to leave the earth. The dog stood beside me, and I thought, Pete, you've got gray in your muzzle and you're slower than the last time I saw you. Travis and Damien are going to have a hard time losing you. But everything brought into the world is taken out again.

I read the Bible for a class in college. I also read philosophy, history, literature, psychology, and science. I don't mean just what I was assigned, but whatever I could find in addition. That's how you got educated, I believed, outside of what you were taught, outside of what you were supposed to learn. You read in order to figure out what questions to ask, never mind if you couldn't find the answers.

"When will the funeral be?" I said.

"That hasn't been determined yet," Sam said. "It will be a private Catholic service in Holbrook. The mother wants it that way."

"That seems selfish."

"It's her right to be selfish," Sam said. "It's her decision."

In a strong wind we walked back along the wash, and I looked to the south at the small houses and mobile homes of Black Canyon City, the town split in half by the interstate, with Mud Springs Road running underneath it like a river. I used to describe the town to Jody and explain to her about Lee and his second family, where they lived and what they did and how old the boys were and what we did together and where I stayed, when I was there. I used to think about Lee's family a lot—what he had versus what I had. I think it's natural to want whatever has been put in front of you. "Once you find Hannah," I used to tell Jody, "she can live here with us and we'll call us a family." I pictured the three of us in my RV, with Jody and me together as a couple, maybe married. It was the first thought I had when I found out she was dead—that my dreams were gone. It was like I missed them, at first, almost more than I missed her. Everybody comes with attachments.

BACK AT THE house, in the patio chairs under the corrugated roof, Sam Rush asked me questions and told me about the photograph Mike Early had of Jody in his robe. I hadn't known about it and it shocked me and I tried to act as if it hadn't. But I knew better than anyone how many men were attracted to Jody, and I also knew that she knew that and used it. I might have told Sam that if he were not so hard on her, not so judgmental and cold. I could have told him about the men at the restaurant who watched her, stared at her as she came out from behind the counter and crossed the room. One of them stalked her for a month—followed her to the RV and drove past it daily, she said, until I happened to be there, one afternoon, and he saw me. Another customer had seemed decent and kind to her, at first. She had become friendly with him, just as she had become friendly with me, and one afternoon she walked outside with him and got into his car—a new red Altima, she said it was. She sat in his car because it was cold outside and she told him about Hannah and what a private detective would cost and he said, "Let me help you," and he gave her $50, and the next day he came into the restaurant and said he would give her another fifty if she would sit in his car again. She considered it, she told me. She said that for five minutes it didn't occur to her that he could speed off in the car with her in it. The possibility just didn't come into her mind.

That was how Jody was—naive and a little unintelligent. And maybe, for reasons I didn't understand, she looked for trouble. Plus she knew how to utilize her looks. She'd adjust her smile depending on the kind of man she was waiting on. I would tell her, "You don't have to make a prostitute of yourself to make a living," and she would say, "It's not called being a prostitute. It's called being a waitress." When it came to that subject and many others, I would try and explain my point of view to her, which she wasn't interested in hearing. If my thoughts didn't agree with hers, she was certain I was wrong. She just assumed it. It was irritating, as it would have been for anybody. I was smarter than she was, and she couldn't see it. But I was also sorry for her because of it. It was complicated, how we were with each other. I could never simplify it to myself.

She was sad a lot of the time. If we were having a rum and Coke together, she would start to talk about Hannah and want more to drink so that she could feel sadder still—that was how it seemed to me. She

told me about her mother becoming an addict, and about how she—
Jody—started stealing a few pills, then a few more. She told me about
her father leaving them for a woman who ended up trying to stab him
at a Burger King with a plastic knife. Jody would laugh when she got to
that part of the story, then she would cry when she got to the ending,
which was that a year after the woman abandoned her father, her father
had a heart attack and died and four days went by before anybody
found him. Four days, she said.

I tried to respect Jody's emotions even if that meant forgetting my
own. I asked her how she felt and pretended to listen to the long answers.
Sometimes resentment dug a hole in me, and it was difficult not to fall
into it since I used to do all right, living by myself—not happy, but not
lonely. It's the crowd that makes you lonely. I was all right with the life
I had, not expecting more, not mourning what I didn't have or hadn't
had in the past. But most of the time, with Jody, I sidestepped resentment and was kinder to her than anybody else had been. And I tried to
teach her things.

Ernest Sterling said that every moment of your life you should
think about the fact that you weren't dead. Like when you were eating
a hot dog or barreling down a highway, you should remember, *Life. I
have it*, and not ask for anything more. When I said that to Jody she
said she would kill herself, thinking that way. She would want to kill
herself every minute; why would I put a thought like that in her head?
She couldn't see that I was trying to help her. She couldn't see that there
was another way to look at your life and another way to feel. It was like
she refused to think deeply or use her imagination.

She had a childish side that pulled at you when she was sitting
alone with her feet tucked under her, or when she was standing quietly

for a moment, at a window. You would wonder what her thoughts were and you would imagine what she was feeling, and for some reason you would lose track of the fact that you couldn't know. You couldn't know with anyone.

At night I was affected by the fact that she was sleeping behind a thin partition twelve feet from me. I would lie on the futon and masturbate like I used to at home when I was in middle school. If Jody was aware of what I was doing, she never said. It would have embarrassed both of us, and there wasn't that kind of closeness between us anyway. She didn't want it and maybe she didn't know how to do it and neither did I. It might not be enough to want to. You might have to make room for it in yourself, set aside some of you for some of it. Then you would have to get used to that new configuration. So I left Jody alone when it came to my sexual feelings. I was afraid of looking like one of those jerks who wanted things from her, and I thought that when she was ready she would come around to me. Only, the longer I waited the longer it didn't happen.

In the afternoon we sat together on the steps of the RV. Each RV was set into a private island of eucalypts and pine. Beyond the trees you could see the narrow, white-gravel roads that wound through the park. They were like paths in a fairy tale, Jody said, like you'd expect them to take you someplace good. Her hair was longer then, falling to her shoulders. It was soft and dark against her white sweatshirt. We would watch the light dying, and if Jody was cold, she would say, "Put your arms around me, Nate," and we would sit that way. We would sit that way long past sunset.

chapter eight

TRAVIS ASPENALL

NOBODY COULD HAVE predicted it, my father said, that much rain in April—enough for Tonto Creek to flood with five families from Black Canyon City camping alongside it. Four children washed away. It was in the newspaper and on television; and in English class on Monday, when Mr. Drake read to us, *Stars, I have seen them fall, / But when they drop and die / No star is lost at all / From all the star-sown sky,* Selena Maynard started crying and it turned out that she used to babysit for one of those drowned children. Mr. Drake walked her down to the nurse's office. We were pretty much silent while he was gone. We didn't look at each other. Some people went so far as to look at their books.

"I wish I had never done anything with Selena," Billy said to Jason and me after class. "Now I feel like a creep."

"That's because you are a creep," Jason said.

The three of us joked around all the time, but it wasn't like we didn't know we felt things.

In Honors Physical Science, third period, when we were supposed to be talking about the periodic table, we talked about global warming instead—what the phrase meant and what some scientists said had caused it and what people on the other side of the argument said. Ms. Hanson said that she believed global warming was what was happening to the Earth, although it was impossible to prove, and that most scientists believed it, and Harmony Cecil said that the Earth was getting too small for the kinds of people who lived on it.

"What does that mean?" somebody in the back row said.

"Greedy people don't give a shit about whether the Earth is polluted," Harmony told him.

"Does that sentence need a four-letter word?" Ms. Hanson said.

"I think it does," I said, and Harmony smiled at me.

She sat in the window aisle in a blue shirt and a jean skirt, with a cuff bracelet on her wrist. She was wearing sandals and she slipped her feet out of them. Her toenails were painted a pinkish color. Her legs were bare and her skin was gold and smooth. I couldn't concentrate on what was happening to the Earth. I couldn't care about it. It was like Harmony was the wind pushing every other thought aside.

SEVENTH PERIOD WAS cancelled that afternoon, and we were asked to gather in the gymnasium. We didn't have to go, the principal said over the intercom, but it was an important decision and we should think about it before we decided. We should think about the meaning of community and what life would be like if everybody were self-interested instead of generous. So we all understood we had to go.

I sat in the bleachers with Harmony, making it look as if it had just happened, as if I had been headed in that direction anyway, and she said, "Oh, hey," as if she hadn't suspected anything different. She was drawing a picture on her hand between her thumb and index finger, of what looked like a spider web, then she looked down at the center of the basketball court, below us, where the principal and vice principal were standing with the counselor. The counselor started speaking into a microphone. He told us that when a sad and tragic thing has happened, people should come together. We should come together and think about those four children even if we hadn't known them, and we should think about their families.

"We're going to have three minutes of silence," he said, "during which we can express our feelings silently in our own way."

Most of us looked at the floor and waited for the time to be up, thinking our own thoughts. Mine were about how Jody Farnell had looked when Damien and I had found her. It's hard to describe what it's like, seeing a dead person. It's as if they're not inside their body anymore, and you try to imagine what they had been like alive and you can't, even though in my case I half-remembered Jody Farnell as a waitress. And as much as you don't want to keep looking at the body, you do; you can't help yourself. You're looking at how you're going to be one day. How everybody will. You're thinking, How can that be real? But it is real. It's in front of you. So you can't stop looking because you're trying to convince yourself.

When the three minutes of silence were up the counselor said that he and Ms. Deakin and Mr. Hollis would stay until five in case anybody wanted to talk to them privately. Hardly anybody did.

INSTEAD OF HARMONY and I getting on our buses, we called home, made excuses, and walked down to Byler's on Old Black Canyon Highway. We stood in the parking lot in the wind and sun, watching a dust devil spin and jump and skip far off in the desert. Then we got take-out Cokes and walked up to High Desert Park and sat on a picnic table with our feet on the bench.

The interstate was below us, and to the west were the mountains. Between the park and the interstate was Community Cemetery, and we looked down at the gravestones, which seemed tiny from where we sat, miniature gravestones in a miniature cemetery. We made up sayings we wanted to have put on ours, such as, *Just Visiting*, which was mine, and *Looks Better with Makeup*, which was hers, even though Harmony didn't wear makeup as far as I could see. But Nate had told me that all girls wore it, that if they put it on well enough you could be fooled completely, which was the point of it. I used to believe most of what Nate told me, and I realized suddenly that I didn't anymore, and I wasn't sure when I had stopped.

"Are you afraid of dying?" Harmony asked me.

"No. Not really."

"Me either. There's too many things to do first."

"No kidding," I said.

When I saw that she had said it seriously, I asked, "Like what?" and she said, "Well, stuff after high school, like going to college or whatever, but also some things now. Smaller things."

We were sitting close enough that our shoulders were touching, and I took a chance and said, "I feel the same way," and I put my arms around her and kissed her. At first I could tell that she hadn't done it much before, but soon it was as if she had always known how, and while I could have tried to do more, I didn't. I would wait for next time. I would give her time to hope I would.

I didn't know how long we had been there until I heard the cactus wrens and quail start up, the way they did early and late in the day, and in the middle of kissing part of a poem from English class came into my mind: . . . *that time allows / In all his tuneful turning so few and such morning songs.* I thought about telling Harmony. I wanted to show her that I remembered it word for word, that I was sensitive like she was, that I had a poetic soul or whatever, which I probably didn't, and which she probably knew. She was as smart or smarter than I was. It was safer to keep it to myself.

chapter nine

SAM RUSH

T HE DAY BEFORE Jody Farnell's landlord was due back in Winslow, I drove up to Flagstaff to the Hilton Inn where Jody had worked and spoke to the assistant manager, a heavyset woman with cropped hair. She knew of nobody problematic in Jody's life, although Jody had been overly chatty with the male clientele at first; the other maids had commented on it, felt she was doing it in order to receive tips. The assistant manager's take was that Jody was lonely, a little troubled, maybe, but well-meaning. She had a talk with Jody about it; that was all it took. Moreover one of the male guests turned out to be her uncle. "A big, white-haired man with glasses," the assistant manager said. "I believe he stayed with us just the one time. That was back in March."

Overall, the assistant manager told me, Jody was a diligent employee who seldom missed work, and they were sorry to hear what had happened to her and sorry to lose her.

FROM FLAGSTAFF I made the forty-five-minute drive to Winslow and had lunch at Bojo's on Second Street, the restaurant Nate had mentioned to me. The manager said that Jody had eaten there once or twice a week, including the day I was asking about, April 24, the last day of her life. She had eaten lunch there, he said, with a white-haired man in his sixties, whom he identified from the photograph I showed him of Mike Early.

"You're certain?" I said.

"Yeah, I'm certain. I paid attention. It was obvious he wasn't her grandfather, if you know what I mean."

In the afternoon I made the drive to Chino Valley and was waiting for Mike Early at his RV when he came home from work. It was breezy and cool, with the sun behind the trees.

Early, a big-headed man with carefully parted white hair politely asked me in, as he had last time. He was a large man, an inch or two under my height. He took the chair opposite me. His RV was paneled, which made the interior dim, despite the overhead light. The photograph of Jody, I noticed, was no longer in sight.

"As I told you on the phone," I said, "it appears that you and Nate both got the date wrong about when you had that water leak."

"Well, I don't have the best memory," he said. "I've said that."

"The odd thing was that your dates matched. You both told the same story. Why do you think that was?"

"I don't know. Coincidence, maybe."

"Can you see how that looks to me," I said, "two people alibiing each other? I'm not saying that you were both somehow involved. I'm just saying I have to consider it, especially since you each had a relationship with her."

"Not the kind you're thinking of. Neither of us did."

"How do you know that?"

"Jody told me," he said. "She offered that information to me."

"Nate cared for her. You must have known that. Would he have been jealous of you or any man who had relations with her?"

"Maybe," Early said.

"Would he have been angry at her?" I asked.

"I don't know. I can't say. I don't know him in that capacity."

"Then let's focus on you for a minute," I said. "Where were you the night Jody was killed? Your neighbor said you didn't come home all night. She said she was sure of it."

He took off his tie and lay it carefully over his leg. "What I did," he said slowly, "was confuse Thursday with Friday. I realized that finally. I have a sister and brother-in-law in Snowflake, and I thought it was Friday night I spent with them, when in fact it was Thursday night."

"After going to Winslow to see Jody," I said.

He was silent, surprised. He averted his eyes and smoothed the tie with his big fingers.

"The manager at Bojo's said that Jody had a late lunch there, the day she was killed, with a white-haired man in his sixties, who was seen getting out of a pickup that matches yours in make and color. He identified you from a copy of the photo on your driver's license."

Early removed his glasses, looked down at them as he spoke.

"She asked me to come," he said. "She called me earlier in the week, saying she didn't have anyone in Winslow except her mother, who had pneumonia. She might be dying, Jody said. Then there were other issues. Somebody was knocking on Jody's bedroom window late at night, and calling, then hanging up. She didn't know who. Plus there was her landlord, who had offered to drop her rent in return for sex. And she was nervous about the father of her child. She hadn't found him yet, but maybe he had heard she was looking for him and why, and didn't want to give the child back. Jody said she needed to see somebody she could depend on, and that if I could come visit soon, she'd . . ."

"What?"

"Be . . . grateful."

"In a sexual way? She'd have intercourse with you?"

"No. A lesser thing," he said. "I don't like to say. I don't use those words. I'm not comfortable . . ."

"She would perform oral sex on you."

"Yes."

"She had done that before?"

He looked at the paneled wall, on which was hanging a picture of a bright-faced young man in a red polo shirt.

"It happened just once," he said, "shortly before she left Chino Valley."

"She suggested it, or you did?"

"I lent her money and she wanted to thank me. She said, 'I'll do such-and-such.'" He sagged forward, forearms on his thighs. "I wouldn't have asked. You don't know me. I'm not like that."

"What about the time you stayed at the Hilton Inn in Flagstaff, where Jody was working? What did the two of you do then?"

He avoided looking at me.

"It was just . . . well, it didn't amount to much . . . I was trying to help her out."

"With money?"

"Yes."

"For which she paid you back in sex," I said.

"It wasn't that type of arrangement. I don't like the way that makes either of us sound."

"Leaving aside how it sounds, Mr. Early, do you know if she had this kind of arrangement with any other man, or men?"

"No. I can't believe she did."

"Why is that?" I said.

"Because come to think about it, it might have been my suggestion. I'll just go ahead and say that now." Early looked out his window. The sun was down and there were glimpses of red sky behind the trees. "The friendship we had was the basis for it," he said. "Jody was warm. Sweet. She'd hug me hello and I felt our relationship was . . . loving, I suppose you would say. I thought maybe she saw it in the same light."

"Did Nate know anything about the sexual aspect of your relationship?" I said.

"No. Not so far as I know."

"So why did she want you in Winslow on the twenty-fourth," I said, "rather than the two of you seeing each other in Flagstaff, as you had before?"

"She sounded, well, nervous, alone. Wanted to see a friendly face in Winslow. That was my impression. She was on edge."

"Where and when did the oral sex with Jody take place?"

He kept his eyes on the floor as he spoke.

"It was after lunch," he said. "We drove separately to the overlook for the Painted Desert, on the Reservation. She got into my truck and we drank some. I had stopped at the liquor store earlier. Then after a while, she . . . well, it happened, and before she left I gave her $300. To help her, Deputy Sheriff, whether you believe that or not. Then she got into her car—this would have been at four or so. And I drove down to Snowflake, where my sister and brother-in-law live. I got there at suppertime and spent the night. I can give you their phone number."

I said, "What about this man Jody was afraid of? Did she say any-thing else about him that day?"

"That she saw him once, for a second. He was in his thirties or for-ties, she said, about the same age as her landlord."

"Her landlord is seventy-one."

"It's easy for young people to get ages wrong," Early said.

"Yes it is. But usually they err in the opposite direction."

"Well, she was afraid of somebody," he said. "Probably more than one somebody. Jody could . . . sometimes it was hard to tell with her. But she didn't invent it. There was always a truth underneath."

"Does Nate know you were in Winslow that day, or that she asked you there?"

Early glanced in the direction of Nate's RV.

"No," he said. "I wouldn't like him to . . . I'm not sure what he would think."

"Just how well do you know Nate?" I asked. "How much has he told you about his family? For example, his father's second family and where they're located?"

"Well, he told me that his mother's in Prescott. I believe his father lives in Black Canyon City, or near Black Canyon City. Out in the des-ert a ways, Nate said. Nate has half brothers. He's told me that, too, although I've never met them."

"What about Jody? Did she talk at all about Nate's family? Where the father lived? Anything like that?"

"Never mentioned them," Early said.

IN MY SUV, five minutes later, I called Mike Early's sister and brother-in-law. They said that Early had arrived at suppertime, on April 24, and spent the night. However they lived fifteen miles outside of town and didn't have neighbors. They were afraid there were just the two of them to verify it.

"How long did Mike stay with you?" I asked. It was the sister I was speaking to.

"He left fairly early the next morning. He didn't spend the day with us, as we had been hoping."

chapter ten

NATE ASPENALL

T HE FIRST TIME you see a girl you care for, naked, well, you know basically what to expect, physically, but you don't have any idea about seeing the heart inside the body, by which I mean the inside of a person suddenly appearing along with the outside. You get an erection at the same time that you see the fragility of a human being, the soul in a person, if you want to put it that way. It had never happened to me; I had never cared for a girl that much. It made me want to protect her from whatever could hurt her—pain and sickness; growing old; herself, maybe; men who didn't love her; and a child she might never see again.

It had been an accident, my walking in midmorning as she was stepping out of the shower, the sunlight from the window on her small, pretty breasts, on the whiteness of her stomach and legs. She wrapped herself in a towel, and I said, "Sorry," and went outside to give her privacy and take hold of myself. Her body was in my head now—how it looked and what I felt and the whole effect of it.

This happened in December, and from that moment on I was magnetized to her, whether we were in the RV, or at Denny's with her waiting on me, or at the grocery store, or in my pickup as I was giving her a ride to or from work—saving her gas money, was the excuse I used. "Let me help, Jody. I have errands to run anyway. Really, I don't mind." I was nervous when I couldn't see her—jittery, as if I were in withdrawal. My time away from her was spent waiting until I could see her again.

I started thinking of her as this rare bird who had flown into my possession and was my sacred responsibility. Who else but me could show her the safest route? She had come to me naked, and I understood what she didn't: the darkness within ourselves, the shortness and loneliness of life, the unknown that awaited us. It was up to me to protect her and make her wise, give her what nobody else could or would.

I told her that people believed in the world too much, with its stores and lights and restaurants, and she should wean herself away from that. I explained that the world was outer, like the skin of a balloon, and people were inner, like the air inside, which was oxygen and nitrogen, meaning it had substance, that there was no nothing. There wasn't a vacancy we had to fill.

"I don't care, Nate," she said. "I don't even know what you're talking about."

We were in the parking lot of the Prescott Mall, where she had wanted to go. I couldn't talk her out of it, couldn't persuade her that the mall was a fantasy that she should let go of. But ultimately we went in, and I followed her from one store to another, where she couldn't afford anything, she told me. How was it everybody else could? What was the fairness in that? Then on the way home she grew teary; she told me that she and her mother used to shop in Flagstaff at the thrift stores. This was when Jody was eleven or so. They would drive there and back listening to her mother's music from the eighties, and afterward they would drive past the house Jody's father had moved into with the woman who ended up stabbing him with a plastic knife. They didn't go up and knock or anything, Jody said, but sat in the car across the street from the house—a shotgun house, Jody said, no bigger than a trailer, with peeling paint and a faded pelican statue stuck in the yard, as if whoever had put it here—Jody's father or the woman with the knife or somebody else entirely—had not figured out that the ocean was a state and half of desert away.

Jody's mother would smoke and look at the house and be silent, and Jody would be counting one, two, three, four, she said, as far up as she could stand, then she'd sing songs in her mind, or think of a boy—whatever it took for her to survive that time in the car with her mother without remembering when her parents had been together and she had had a family.

When you cared for somebody, you got caught up in her story; it became more real than your own. For it wasn't as if I didn't have my own. The day my father, Lee, left, his car caught fire. Whether Sandra torched it, or he torched it himself, for some reason, I never knew—the two of them could get crazy with each other, they each told me later, as if I didn't remember the flames, the sirens, Sandra screaming, and black smoke billowing up. I was five or so. For a long time I would dream that day and wake up choking.

Your long-ago past collides with your present. For no clear reason I'll find myself thinking about three people I knew in high school who considered suicide on a daily basis. Truthfully, two of them would not have been missed, but the one who would have was the one to do it.

He and I used to skip class to smoke pot behind the Phippen Museum and watch the reflection of clouds as they sailed along in those plate-glass windows. Or else we would drive out to the Ernest A. Love Field and watch the small planes take off and land. After graduation we were going to join the military together, for him to be a pilot and me to be in tanks. A daydream, really—a castle in the air. He hanged himself from an upper branch of a cottonwood tree. He used to say that if he had been born somebody else, he could have helped out the person who had been him, but that as it was, he had only the one of him, and it wasn't enough. But his thinking wasn't always that dark, and if he hadn't died, I believe we might have remained friends.

Everybody's life gets peppered with losses. That's what I tell myself. But I see it the other way, too, by which I mean I see what my friend lost, and I see what Jody lost. I don't forget that part. I don't think it's all or only about me.

chapter eleven

TRAVIS ASPENALL

"I SEE THIS IS a birthday dinner," Nate said. He didn't smile. There wasn't emotion in his voice. He wished we had forgotten.

He sat at the table wearing the Grateful Dead T-shirt that had once belonged to Dad. Mom put a plate of chicken-fried steak and mashed potatoes in front of him—the meal he ordered when we went to Byler's Amish Kitchen. Nobody said anything about Sam Rush not being present. Whether or not my mother had invited him I didn't know, but his not being there felt stranger than it would have been if he had come. Normally on birthdays he was with us.

Damien and I had made a CD for Nate—"Purple Haze," "Black Magic Woman," "Stairway to Heaven," "Gimme Shelter," "Born to Be Wild," and so on, the only music Nate listened to. My parents had given him a Kindle and shouldn't have. Nate didn't get excited by what you could do with an iPhone, and he had never been on Facebook or Twitter or anything. He needed to stand apart, and I guess that was how he chose to do it. If he were running a race, I thought, he would try to be the slowest.

After supper Damien and I cleared the table, and my mother brought out the cake. She lit the candles, and Damien said, "Aren't we going to sing?"

"No," Nate said. "Let's just eat."

My mother sliced the cake, and Nate ate a piece, then a second one. We were quiet because he was. He had worked with my father, that day, at the veterinary clinic, which my father had started asking him to do—to get him out of the Airstream, my mother said. It bothered her and Dad that he spent so much time alone.

"Next year's birthday will be better, Nate," Dad said. They were sitting at either end of the table. Our kitchen and dining room were combined into one rectangle, with yellow walls and a wood floor.

"Better in what way?" Nate said.

"Let's hope in every way."

"You might have a new girlfriend next year," Damien said.

"I might," Nate said. "I might have one who likes me better."

"How come Jody didn't?" Damien said.

"Don't ask personal questions," Mom said.

"Sometimes girls don't like you back," Nate said.

"What didn't she like about you?"

"I don't think it was any one thing."

"Who did she like?"

"It was hard to tell."

"Maybe nobody," Damien said.

"Yes," Nate said. "That's possible."

NATE AND DAMIEN and I cleaned up, despite my mother saying "Don't help, Nate. Really. It's your birthday. You shouldn't have to."

He nodded his head slightly to signal that he had heard her. But he didn't pay attention. He filled the sink with water and got to work. He washed the dishes slowly and with concentration while I stood next to him, drying. He didn't talk at all. It was like he was a worker in a restaurant.

When he finished he got the broom from the closet and swept the floor. "Dog hair," he said, as if that were our fault.

Instead of going back to the Airstream he got a beer and went outside with us. My father watched him drink it. Dad worried that we were going to become alcoholics someday, since he had been one, or, as he put it, still was one; he went to AA meetings twice a week. He was often warning us about it.

"I appreciate your spending time with us tonight," Dad said to Nate. Dad was in a patio chair, and Nate was cross-legged on the concrete, a few feet away.

"Are you being sarcastic?" Nate said.

"I'm being serious."

"I can't always tell," Nate said.

"Am I usually sarcastic with you? Is that what you think? Maybe you misinterpret my tone."

"Everybody hears things differently," Nate said.

"I don't intend to be sarcastic, Nate. Intention has to count for something."

"Maybe so," Nate said.

"We're together for your birthday," Mom said. "I'm glad for that."

Nate drank his beer without looking at us. It was almost dark by then. He hadn't been this quiet a person before now. He used to talk in rushes. He would get on what my father would call a rant about one thing or another—usually some philosophical subject, such as how you

should live your life away from the crowd, or why you should be suspi-
cious of anything that managed to find its way into print. His quietness
used to come only at intervals. But now it had taken over. We were all
sitting right there near him, but it was as if he were sitting there alone.

LATER, I WENT with the dog in the direction of Billy's mother's house.
She and Billy's father were divorced, and Billy and his sister lived with
their mother during the week and with their father on the weekends.
His father lived a mile away, near Black Canyon Creek, in a house
that had an open feel to it. He was more or less a hippie. Billy and his
sister could do what they wanted within reason, and so could I, including drinking. "One apiece," his father had told us last Saturday. "Any
more and the two of you will be drunk on your asses."

We were sitting outside, watching his father teach Dennie how to
run hurdles. There was something hilarious about it. I came close to
telling Billy about what was going on with Nate. Billy had seen Nate's
pickup more than once. He had asked about it. I pictured myself telling
him to see the look on his face and so that we could make jokes about
how weird the situation was.

But in the end I didn't tell him. I knew I couldn't. If I hadn't been
used to keeping things to myself, it would have been harder. But I had
always been the kind of person to listen and not say a lot.

Pete started lagging behind, and I walked him back. The moon
was rising, and it created a milky path across our property. When we
passed the Airstream I could hear Nate's television going, as I always
could at night and early in the morning. Nate kept it on all the time. He
had always been that way. He couldn't sleep without company. He was
lonely in some way I didn't understand.

chapter twelve

SAM RUSH

P AUL BOWMAN WAS a broad man in suspenders, with deep-set eyes and a fleshy face, who had had a heart bypass in January, his wife told me, and was trying to quit smoking. But he smoked as I sat with them in their kitchen in Winslow. Mary Bowman, who was short and big-breasted, with bright blue eyes, made coffee.

"We hardly knew the girl," Bowman said, "but here's what I can tell you. She responded to an ad we put in the paper, and I met her there, at the house. It's about five blocks north of here. She asked if I could reduce the rent by $50, and I said no, and she said she'd think about whether or not she could afford it and let me know. Meanwhile I came home and told my wife and she said . . . well, she can tell you herself what she said."

"I knew her mother a long time ago," Mary Bowman said. "We used to run into each other at the Laundry Mat." She smiled. "That's what it's called. You can see the name for yourself on the side of the building. Anyway, we each had a small child, and we talked about them, how tiring it was, how you feared they'd hurt themselves. Lisa Farnell was younger than I was, and there was something sad about her and I could never figure out what. Then years and years later, when I heard she was into the drugs, I thought, well, that sadness must have taken her there."

"You're getting off the subject," her husband said.

"Yes. I do that," she said to me.

"The point is," Bowman said, "that Mary told me to lower the rent, so I did."

"You argued with me first," Mary said.

"True. But I told Jody she could have the house for $350 instead of $400, utilities included, and she thanked me for that. She said it would help."

"She didn't want to move in with her mother," Mary said. "There were the drugs, and the fact that her mother's trailer was too small for two people, let alone three, if you include the child Jody was due to get back."

"You spoke to Jody yourself?" I said. "And she told you this detail about the child?"

"Yes. Once, when she came by to pay the rent. Generally I don't get to know the tenants. We have three other rentals, and Paul is the one who keeps them up and rents them out. I just do the bookkeeping. Anyway, I spoke to her only that one time, and that was what she told me."

"We weren't here the night she was killed," Bowman said. "You know that already. We had left on our trip a few days before that, and we didn't hear about the murder until our neighbor called and said a Navajo County deputy sheriff was looking for us. Where was it we were the night she was killed, honey?" he asked his wife.

"Albuquerque." Mary rummaged through a drawer and handed me a receipt from a Comfort Inn. "Our daughter lives in Amarillo, and we visit as often as we can. She has three little girls. I keep saying to Katie, 'Move back here so we can see more of you and the children.' But there's Roy, who doesn't want to come back, even though he could get a job in Flagstaff. He's got something against us."

"You're going on again," Bowman told her.

"I'm telling you things you don't care to know," Mary said to me. "I see that. How about if I just pour you more coffee? Would you like a second cup?" I nodded and she poured me one and I waited for her to sit again.

"What else did Jody say about being due to get her child back?" I asked.

"Nothing," Mary said. "Just that one sentence. I remembered it, because while I knew there was a child, I had heard that she—wasn't it a girl?—was with the father, and that they had moved away from Winslow years ago. I don't think anybody knew where they were."

"How is it you know about him and the child?"

"This is Winslow," Mary said. "It's small. You hear things. On top of that, I used to be in a quilting group with Alice Weneka. She's the woman who took in the boy who fathered Jody's baby. She took him in after his mother died. I believe her daughters were friends with him. Alice said that he—Wes Giddens, his name was—moved away with the baby. He needed a new start, she said."

"Why was that?"

"Well, his mother had died here in Winslow, and his father was in prison. Wes hardly knew his dad, was what Alice said, but a lot of people were aware of it."

"What kind of person was Wes?"

"Smart, according to Alice. Hoped to be a nurse someday, like she was. Alice was a nurse at the Indian Clinic. Maybe she still is, it's been so long since I've seen her."

Mary looked up at the clock, took a pill from a container on the counter, and drew a glass of water for her husband.

"As far as you know," I said, "he hasn't moved back here?"

"Not that I've heard," Mary said.

"What about other people in Jody's life? Did either of you ever see Jody out and about?"

"No," Bowman said. "As we told you, we hardly knew her. She moved in, with the little she had. She paid the rent on time, or close to on time."

"The Navajo County deputy sheriff took me through the house," I said, "but I'd like to see it again. You mind driving over there with me?"

Bowman seemed not to have expected that. But he got up from his chair and followed me out to my SUV. It was a cool, bright day, and he squinted at the sunlight.

"So you visited the house after she was living in it?" I said on the drive over. "That's how you knew she didn't have many possessions?"

"I went over to replace the shower nozzle," he said. "That was three weeks or so before my wife and I left for our trip. Jody called and asked me to, and I did."

"What did the two of you talk about?" I said.

"The shower nozzle."

"That's all?"

"What are you asking?"

"I'm asking, was Jody flirtatious with you, or you with her?"

I pulled up in front of the rental, which was a small, plain, white house without shutters. The grass in front was sparse—sandy dirt, more than anything. Bowman looked at the house for a minute or two before speaking.

"She was a pretty girl," he said. "When I first showed her the house and she asked if I could lower the rent she had looked at me in a certain way. I didn't want to say that in front of my wife. But I knew that look and what it meant, and I didn't say or do anything by way of response. I just told her no, like I mentioned earlier. I'm telling you the truth now. I know it's important."

We got out of the SUV and went into the rental. Bowman walked slowly, either from reluctance or the state of his health. Jody's belongings were just as she had left them. Only after the investigation was concluded would they be given to Jody's mother, should she want them.

"There was a photograph here," he said, pointing to the table beneath the living room window. "I saw it the day I replaced the shower nozzle. It was a picture of a young man standing in front of one of those recreational vehicles. He was on the small side, thirty or so, with longish, dark hair."

"How is it you remember that so well?"

"Jody saw me looking at it. She said, 'That's who I used to live with in Chino Valley. He's my boyfriend, sort of. He's coming up to see me in a few weeks.'"

"Word for word?"

"Yes. I remember wondering if she'd be moving back to Chino Valley with him, and I'd have to rent the place out again. That's why I recall it."

"What else did Jody say about this boyfriend?" I asked.

"Nothing else."

"Not his name, for example? Or his family?"

"No. Although she was talkative," Bowman said. "I can tell you that. She didn't use good judgment in terms of keeping what should be private, private. But I wasn't much interested in the boyfriend, and I didn't act as if I was."

"Well, sometimes people mention things in passing, you know, the name of a town, for example. You recollect Jody saying anything like that?"

"Just that the boyfriend lived in Chino Valley."

When we were back in my SUV I showed him a copy of Nate Aspenall's driver's license, and he said, "Yes. That's him, I believe, the fellow in the picture."

"How about this man?" I said. "Have you seen him before?" I showed him a photocopy of Mike Early's driver's license.

"No. He's not familiar to me."

"What other information can you give me about Jody that would be easier to say here, away from your wife?"

He hesitated, his face shiny with sweat, despite the coolness of the afternoon. "The day I replaced that nozzle," he said, "after she told me about the boyfriend, or whoever he was to her, she asked if she could call me if she ever needed help. 'Help with what?' I said, and she said, 'With anything, because you never know what could happen.' I said, 'Well, I'm the landlord, so if it's related to the house, sure, call me,' and she said, 'Can I call you if it's not related to the house?'

"I didn't know what to say. I thought about Mary and what she might think. I thought about the fact that Jody could have been in some kind of trouble, that maybe she was trying to tell me that. Then, as I was standing there, before I said a word, she unbuttoned her sweater and took it off and removed her bra. Just stood in front of me like that, half naked, and I said, 'You'd best call the police, if that's the kind of thing you're talking about,' and I got out of there as fast as I could. To tell you the truth, it was creepy to me."

"And you didn't tell your wife."

He looked at the wide, windswept street, at the end of which a train was passing on the Santa Fe Rail Line. "I cheated on my wife once," he said. "She said she would leave me next time, and there hasn't been one. She wouldn't have believed the story about Jody, that I hadn't asked for it somehow, or hadn't acted on what Jody was offering me. You probably don't believe me yourself."

"Let's go back a bit. What do you mean, creepy? Why did you have that response?"

"Jody was young. And small as she was, she looked younger still. I have a daughter and granddaughters, Deputy Sheriff. I may have cheated on my wife, but it wasn't with a kid or somebody who resembled one."

"Did Jody ever call you after the conversation?" I asked.

"No."

"Did she ever mention being afraid of anybody?"

He shook his head.

"Has anybody ever owned this rental besides you? Or rented it out on your behalf?"

"I bought it from an elderly man who had lived there most of his life," Bowman said. "That was fifteen years ago. And nobody has ever rented it out but me."

When I pulled up to his house I saw his wife watching from the living room window, looking relieved to see her husband coming up the walkway.

IT WAS AFTER eight when I returned to Black Canyon City, and I had supper at the Rock Springs Café. Audrey Birdsong waited on me. A year and a half ago, before her husband, Carl, had died, they had lived behind me, on Spencer Street. I used to run into the two of them walking at dusk in the neighborhood, before Carl got sick, and we'd stop and talk a minute. I had liked them both. Audrey had a freckled face that was wide at the cheekbones and narrow at the chin, and she resembled Julie Aspenall in terms of her height and long hair.

"Since when are you waitressing?" I said. As far as I knew, she did people's taxes.

"For a while now," she said, "except during tax season. It's not as bad as it looks, Sam, and it keeps me busy, which is good for me. It keeps me from being lonely."

So you're not dating anybody, I wanted to say. But I didn't know what the etiquette was, where a death was concerned, and I didn't want to seem forward or insensitive. What I did say was, "It can be lonely living alone."

"Especially when you're not used to it," she said. "Though you'd think I would be by now."

She smiled with some sadness and I tried to think of something to say and couldn't, and she went to get my supper. As I ate she cleared and set tables for breakfast, and I pretended not to watch her. Then she brought my check, and I paid it, and we spoke a minute more about the warm temperatures starting and how soon we would be complaining. Then we said good night.

My two years of marriage had not been good ones. My wife had had an affair with a man she later married, something she still didn't know I knew. Other than my attraction to Audrey Birdsong, the only woman I found myself drawn to was Julie Aspenall, and that had been going on a long time. I had been with Lee when he first saw her at the Crown King Bar, up in Crown King, and if he hadn't approached her, I would have. It was possible that she knew that. There had been an afternoon, once, close to Christmas, a year after my divorce, when she and I ran into each other at the Cave Creek Trading Post and went next door together to the Mexican restaurant. She showed me her purchases: an old Indian drum for Travis, and so on.

It was dusk when we walked out to the parking area, and she gave me a hug good night and kissed me. The hug wasn't unusual for her but the kiss was. If you were lost in the desert, you would remember your last glass of water for a long time. But it wasn't just that, and I wanted to think that it wasn't any kind of *just* for her, either. Not that anything had or would come of it. I wasn't the kind of person to wreck a friend's marriage, were that possible, and it wasn't. The Aspenalls were happy, at least happier than most married couples I knew. It was just that having a warm, reciprocal connection with a woman didn't happen to me often and it stayed in my mind.

I sat in the Rock Springs Café parking lot, thinking that the restaurant was about to close; soon Audrey would be coming out to her car, and I could ask if she'd be interested in getting together. But the idea of waylaying her made me uncomfortable. If I wanted to ask her out, I should call her, I thought. That was normal behavior. When I got home I would do that, I told myself, yet ten minutes later, at home, I looked up her number, wrote it on a slip of paper, and left it on my kitchen counter. I would wait until the Jody Farnell investigation was over, I decided. I didn't have time for a date now, anyway, which was true, and not just an excuse. Or at least not only an excuse.

chapter thirteen

NATE ASPENALL

J ODY SLEPT DEEPLY. I would get up in the night and stand at the foot of the bed to make sure she was breathing—the comforter rising and falling, the sound of her breath going in and out. It was around New Year's when I started doing that. Maybe I felt I had a right to, since I was taking care of her and since I was patient in terms of what I was hoping would happen between us. Her hair was dark against the white pillowcase and I would put my hand on it, or else I would rest my palm on the slight rise of her breasts under the bedclothes.

I dared myself, I suppose you could say. There was a getting-away-with-something quality to what I was doing, there in the silence, with just the two of us alone in the darkness. I could smell the soap she used, I was standing so close, and I imagined using it on her someday, her asking me to—*Come shower with me, Nate. Let's be naked together.* I believed she would let me do that and more, once she was ready, in whatever way she defined that word. Meanwhile I had this private experience of her, which I would never tell her about, no matter what happened between us. It wasn't hers to know.

Whatever form of sex occurred between two people, there was another, private side that nobody admitted to. That was my belief. It was possible that a lot of men did some version of what I was doing. As for women, I didn't know. My experience was limited to two. The first girl I met in college, and the second I met at the Chino Valley Recreation Center, which was what people like me, who frequented it, called the Highway 89 Tavern, on Havasu Boulevard. The first girl started seeing somebody else, and the second girl, who was from the Philippines, ended up returning to the husband who had mail-ordered her. I used to call the second one after she stopped seeing me. I thought we could continue as friends, if nothing else, unrealistic as that was, needy as that might have seemed to an outsider. I called after she asked me not to. I called until her husband answered her phone and said, "Never call this number again."

I wasn't in love with her or with the first girl either. I didn't care for either of them that much. But at least I got to have sex. I got to hold somebody. I got to belong to that club of which everybody else seemed to be a member.

ON THE FIRST Sunday in January, Jody stayed up with me to watch a meteor shower. We sat on the picnic table, wrapped in blankets; the temperature was near freezing. The moon was shining, and the stars were glittering. We put our heads back, watching one meteor then another carry out its short fall, its flash out of existence.

"Just bits of dust and rock burning up as they enter the atmosphere," I told Jody.

"I thought they were stars, Nate," she said. "I thought I was seeing planets and moons disappear."

She was shivering—we both were—and when we went inside I followed her to bed and got in with her. It seemed natural, cold as we both were. I thought she would see that, somehow, know what I was thinking, know me well enough by then to trust me. Maybe I was testing that trust, or maybe I was just being myself for a change, not twisting myself out of shape in order to put her needs over mine. You didn't always have to have a reason to do what people were meant to do as physical beings, as creatures of the natural world.

"Why are you doing this, Nate?" she said.

"To warm you up, and myself, too. No more than that."

"I don't want you to."

"Just for a few minutes, Jody."

"No."

"I won't touch you," I said. "Look. I'm not touching you now."

"I don't care. I don't want you this close."

"Why not?"

"I just don't," she said. "Not now anyway. Maybe someday but not at this minute."

What choice did I have? But as I disappeared behind the partition I knew as a certainty that she would have said yes if there had been something to gain by letting me stay, or if I were the kind of man who had expected a yes from the beginning and behaved as if I had. I could feel that from her. It was possible that to her I hardly existed.

In the morning she had a headache and a temperature. She took aspirin and drank tea with whiskey. It's medicine, she told me. Watch a Western, Nate. That's what they used it for.

She was sick for three days—the flu, I suppose it was. Her temperature went higher than I thought it would and I waited on her—made her soup, cooled her forehead with a wet washcloth, as my mother used to do with me. That soothed her and made her open up to me. She told me about Winslow and how it happened that she got pregnant.

Wes Giddens had worked at Vince's Auto Repair, she said, down the street from the high school. She would see him as she walked past, this nice-looking, part-Navajo young man who was saving up money to go to college. She would say hello to him, get him talking. He didn't want to go out with her because she was in high school, but he did finally. She talked him into it. It was her idea to have sex, not his. He had resisted at first, which had made him all the more attractive to her. "Plus I thought it would make him like me more," she said. Although by the time she knew she was pregnant he was dating somebody else. "So we weren't together too long," she said, "and there are things I don't remember, due to what I was into, back then."

In grade school she thought she would be famous one day. She would invent something or cure a disease, be a singer or an actress. She wasn't sure when her I'll-be-famous feeling went away, only that when she stopped having it she kept waiting for what would come in its place, and nothing did. She hardly noticed me as she spoke. She was looking beyond me into the past at what she had lost and what she had ruined for herself.

I knew what it was like to make a mistake and not be able to fix it, how it replayed in your head, made you want to reverse time and undo it. I hit a cat in the road once and kept on going. As a kid I pushed a boy off the top of the monkey bars, called an Hispanic kid a greaser, chased a girl off the swings. You do things. You screw up. You are a mystery to yourself. That was what Freud believed, so far as I understood him, and that was a preoccupation in the Bible—all those people who let God down. I mean, there were multitudes.

Ernest Sterling used to have this quotation taped to his dashboard: *Our human life is ten thousand beautiful mistakes.* He couldn't remember where he had come across it, but there it was in front of him every day, and it would come into his thoughts at other times, he said, like when his dog was peeing on somebody's flower bed, or when his toast popped up burned, or when he waited too long to pay his water bill. Then suddenly there it was, he said, those beautiful mistakes that make up a life. "Do you get what I mean, Nate?" he said. And I said no, and he said, "Me neither," and right then, he said, right at that moment of not knowing shit about anything, we were in the midst of it.

AFTER JODY RECOVERED from the flu I had a dream about her. She was sitting on Mike Early's lap, naked, whereas he was clothed. The odd thing was that this was before I knew about the picture, before I knew anything was going on between them. I thought the dream was about how vulnerable Jody was, about how vulnerable maybe everybody was under the surface, no matter what they told you or what their actions were. There was an outside self and an inside, a public and a private, a self they sought to control and a vulnerable self they couldn't. And they tried however they could to make peace between the two.

I was trying to be happier, Hannah, and I went about it wrong. But I was still a good person. I was still trying to be a mother to you.

But all the regrets in the world never saved anybody. I learned that myself. It didn't matter how sorry you were.

chapter fourteen

TRAVIS ASPENALL

H ARMONY CECIL SAT with her friends at lunch, and I sat with mine. There were no rules about it, but nobody moved around much, not from the first or second grade on, even though you could have. Nobody would have stopped you. It was like once you started school you didn't know what freedom was anymore, and that was partly on my mind when I said to Harmony, in the cafeteria, "You could sit with me, you know," and she surprised me by doing it. She sat with me, Billy, and Jason at lunch, instead of with her friends. Her friends sat two tables over, and I noticed her looking toward them as if she were nervous. I wondered if the fact that I had had girlfriends before was something they held against me, or if the fact that I liked Harmony was something they held against her.

Girls were competitive with each other, Nate had told me; you had to watch out for all that jealousy that went on between them. I didn't know then that Nate had never had a real girlfriend, that he was just giving what my father would have called "advice without experience." But he was right about the jealousy, except that it could take a different form, which was that a girl might want *to be* the girl she was jealous of.

I saw that, listening to girls and watching them, and it seemed strange to me, to want to give up your body and never go back, leave your whole self behind as if it didn't count for much.

NEXT TO ME, Harmony was eating her sandwich while Jason and Billy talked to each other instead of to me, as if I had broken some sacred rule by asking a girl to sit with us. Then Harmony said to Jason, "Didn't somebody in your family fight in Iraq?"

"His uncle," Billy said. "His uncle died in Iraq."

"I'm sorry," Harmony said. "I didn't know that part."

"Yeah, well, he went there and didn't come back," Jason said.

"Was he your dad's brother?"

"My mom's," Jason said. "Her younger brother. Well, her only brother."

"What does she think about Afghanistan?"

"She's not in favor of people killing each other."

"It seems crazy to me, too," Harmony said.

"My dad will argue the whole patriotic thing," Jason said, "and on the Fourth of July he'll put the flag up and my mom will take it down and they won't talk to each other for a few days."

"After my brother left for Afghanistan," Harmony said, "my mom burned the flag my dad came home with. Just set it on fire in the trash can, right in front of him, and said, 'Don't you dare,' when he tried to rescue it."

"The war comes to Black Canyon City," Jason said.

"Exactly."

"It never goes away."

"I know," Harmony said. "My brother doesn't want to see us."

"Why is that?"

"I don't know," Harmony said. "I'm not sure. It's like we've done something wrong, only we can't figure out what."

After that we talked about other things, like the empty house down the street from school, where kids went to get stoned; and how screwed up it was that the school secretary was getting fired for being pregnant without having a husband, when everybody knew that the father of the baby was the football coach, who was married, sort of; and why it was that being naked on the Internet was such a big deal, when everybody at every moment was naked under their clothes. But that was mostly just Billy, Jason, and me talking shit, as Billy's father would have called it, fooling around the way we usually did, with Harmony watching us like she had come from another planet in order to check out the earthling males, and was maybe not sure the trip was worth it.

IN ENGLISH CLASS that afternoon Mr. Drake read us a poem, and Harmony sat with one elbow on her desk and her chin in her hand, looking out the window, where clouds were forming shadows on the desert. She had a black headband in her hair, which you could hardly see against the black of her hair. After a few minutes she looked down and followed the poem along in our textbook:

> I let my neighbor know beyond the hill;
> And on a day we meet to walk the line
> And set the wall between us once again.
> We keep the wall between us as we go.

"What is Frost saying about walls?" Mr. Drake said. "Are they good things or bad things?"

"They suck," said somebody.

"Why?"

"Well, the guy in the poem has apple trees, and his neighbor has pine trees," somebody else said, "and trees don't eat each other. So the wall is, like, useless."

"*Something there is that doesn't love a wall,*" Mr. Drake read. "What's the something?" he asked.

"God," said a girl in the front row.

"No, nature," said Harmony. "It proves it by making gaps in the wall."

"Well, it was God who made nature," said the girl.

"God is not in the poem," Harmony said.

"He is there because He made the world and everything in it."

"You're being just like the neighbor," Harmony said. "You want to see things the way you were taught to, instead of thinking for yourself."

"At least that way I'll go to heaven."

"What if there is no heaven?"

"There has to be."

"Why?"

"Okay," Mr. Drake said. "What wall could be erected right now, in our classroom?"

"A wall between people who think one way and people who think the opposite way," said a boy in the second row.

"Does the wall need to be there?" Mr. Drake said.

"It's already there," said somebody else. "We're all, like, fighting with each other. We'll never get along."

"How do you know that?"

"Because it's always been that way."

"Is that what Frost is saying in the poem?" Mr. Drake said.

"Maybe."

"But what is possible for us now," Mr. Drake said, "without a wall in here, that wouldn't be possible if we built an actual wall?"

"Well," another person said, "we could cross the room and kill each other."

"What if we think about this differently? More peacefully?"

"We could walk through the wall," somebody else said, "since it's not there, I mean."

"Yes. What else?" Mr. Drake said. "What happens in the poem?"

"We could walk next to each other," Harmony said.

ON THE BUS home that afternoon, people were screwing around in the aisle and cracking jokes, and the bus driver was half participating and half telling them to shut up and sit down. How was he supposed to pay attention to the road with all that bullshit going on?

Billy was sitting next to me. After a while he told me that his mother was getting married again. He and his sister were being included in the ceremony, and his sister was into it, he said, because she liked the dress she was getting to wear and because she was an idiot. He, himself, was planning on waking up sick and staying home.

"It's bad enough that I'm going to have to live with this asshole," he said.

His mother was marrying Cy Embrick, who owned Ron's Market. Cy was famous for having once lived with a woman who became an actress in X-rated movies, and for setting up folding tables and chairs in the parking lot of his grocery store and serving a free Thanksgiving dinner. But Billy didn't like the idea of his mother having somebody permanent when his father didn't. Plus, his father was sick. His father had cancer—I wasn't sure what kind—and drove to Phoenix once a week for some form of treatment. Billy didn't talk about it, and neither did his father. It was just this thing going on all the time in the background of Billy's life, like rain always falling behind where he stood. I didn't like thinking about it. I had to remind myself, Oh, right. Billy's dad is sick. That's what's going on. Then I'd forget it again and start over.

chapter fifteen

SAM RUSH

"JODY CALLED MIKE Early four days before she was killed," I told Nate. "She asked him to come up there. She told him that somebody was harassing her."

It was shortly after seven, and I had woken Nate up. At the back of the Airstream the bed was unmade.

"She also told Early that her mother was seriously ill," I said. "Jody asked him to come to Winslow, and he did. He had lunch with her the day she died. The waitress identified him."

Nate's face was unexpressive. I had brought two take-out coffees from Byler's and two sausage biscuits, and he started drinking the coffee.

"The afternoon Mike Early was there," I said, "he had a sexual encounter with Jody in his truck. You need to know that."

"Why?"

"Because it happened."

Nate blinked at the early light coming through the window opposite us.

"There must have been a reason," he said. "Maybe he did a favor for her, and she didn't know how else to repay him."

"With sex."

"That was what most men wanted from her."

"So you're not shocked. I thought you might be."

"It doesn't matter what I am," Nate said.

"Why is that?"

"It's not important. What difference can that make now? I don't think Mike was the one to hurt her. Somebody else did, the person she was afraid of, or the landlord, maybe, or Wes Giddens, possibly."

"The landlord was out of town, Nate. I told you that. And for all Jody's talk of Wes Giddens, he wasn't and isn't in northern Arizona, not as far as I can discover. Did Jody tell you she had located him?"

"No. But she wanted her daughter back. She never stopped wanting that."

"I've spoken on the phone to Alice Weneka," I said, "the woman who cared for Wes Giddens after his mother died. She told me that Hannah was born more than a month early, with breathing problems and cocaine and alcohol in her system. Did Jody tell you that?"

Nate touched the wrapping of his sausage biscuit, ran his fingers over the edges of it.

"She told me she had problems, back then," he said. "I knew she took drugs. But she didn't get specific."

"Jody's mother has a picture of Hannah at three months old. Tiny infant, as you can imagine, born that early. That's the only picture she has. Have you seen pictures of Hannah? Did Jody ever show you one?"

"She had a picture of Hannah at about that age," Nate said. "That's the only one I remember. She said that the Navajo family didn't believe in them, and that until Wes and Hannah moved away the Navajo family had the baby most of the time, and that they didn't trust Jody or Jody's mother."

"Since when do present-day Navajos not believe in photographs? I'm just asking," I said.

"Jody could exaggerate," Nate said. "I know that. She could change the truth sometimes in her mind."

"It seems odd, more than odd," I said, "that nobody has a picture of Hannah that's more recent. What I wonder is whether something has since happened to the child."

"If it did, Jody didn't know about it. She wouldn't have lied about something so important to her. And she wasn't living in some other universe, Sam. She wasn't mentally ill, is what I mean. And she had good qualities. She had deep places in herself."

"Doesn't everybody?"

"What is it you're saying?"

"That I think differently than you do," I said. "More factually. For instance, I know that three significant facts about somebody—anybody—can reveal more than you realize."

"What three, where Jody's concerned?"

"She had a baby at a young age, when she was doing drugs, with somebody she hardly knew. I learned that from Alice Weneka. The child never lived with Jody. And these stories about the child being with the father, and Jody being afraid of either him or somebody else, and Jody wanting to get the child back, Jody told to a number of men."

"Which doesn't mean they're not true."

"Or that they are," I said.

"So that's how you see her."

"It's a list, Nate, not an attitude."

I finished my sausage biscuit and took a drink of coffee. Then I said, "I've spoken to the landlord, Paul Bowman, and his wife. They told me a similar story, a story in which Jody talked about the child she was due to get back. In addition, Jody asked Paul Bowman for protection. Asked if she could call him for help."

"You don't believe there was somebody Jody was afraid of? You think she completely made that up?"

"I don't know about completely," I said. "But why were you so quick to believe her, when you knew she could exaggerate?"

Nate was looking out the window at his father walking to his Jeep. Lee and I had played basketball in high school, and he had been quick, wary, and athletic. He was wary now, taking in my SUV. I had brought that on myself by taking on the case, but that didn't make me feel any better about it.

"Jody was more alone in the world than you think she was," Nate said, "despite the men she told stories to, despite me, even. She felt alone. She had this tendency to trust the wrong men. There was somebody from Holbrook she mentioned being nervous about. She probably trusted him some, too, whoever he was. She didn't give me details. But she said she was afraid, and I believed her. The small bird makes the loudest sound."

"Paul Bowman said that Jody mentioned you to him," I said. "Said she had a picture of you standing outside your RV, and that she referred to you as her boyfriend."

That touched Nate. His face softened. It had been some time since I had seen him wear that expression.

"When was that?" he said.

"Three weeks before she was killed. She said you were coming up to see her in a few weeks, which would have put you there close to the week she was killed."

Nate unwrapped his biscuit but didn't eat it.

"Did she ask you to come see her," I said, "the way she had before, when you met her in Flagstaff?"

"No. I offered to come see her, or asked, I guess, and sometimes she would say she wanted me to, and sometimes she would say she didn't. More often it was didn't. Things with Jody changed a lot, depending on her mood or how her mother was." Nate picked up his coffee and took too big a drink. It spilled on his shirt. "She wanted whatever wasn't in front of her. That was what I came to believe. That what she didn't have was what she believed could make her happy. So she was always in a state of . . . I don't know. Longing."

"That's a hard thing to resist in a woman," I said.

"Meaning what?"

"We like to fix things for them, make things better, be the salvation for a woman who will appreciate us and be grateful."

"I gave that a try," Nate said, "October through February. It didn't work very well. But Jody's unhappiness wasn't a game with her, and neither was the wanting what wasn't in front of her. She didn't see it in herself. She couldn't stop and look. She just couldn't. She didn't know how to. Her suffering wasn't an act."

"I know," I said. "That's when it's irresistible."

Nate looked away from me, his face stubborn, but not as if he hadn't understood.

"If you did to go Winslow," I said, "whether on your own or in response to Jody asking you to come, it would be understandable, given that you were worried about her. Anybody could understand that, so long as you tell the truth about it. It's not just me you have to worry about, Nate. I don't work for myself. I report to the Yavapai County Sheriff's Department. On every case I have a county attorney working with me. So it would be best to tell me now."

"Would it?" Nate said, but kept quiet.

NATE ASPENALL

T HERE WAS A girl waitressing at Denny's named Carla Kirby with whom Jody had become friendly. Jody worked the morning shift, six to two, and Carla the two to ten, and often Jody would stay late, helping Carla set tables, fill salt and pepper shakers, fold napkins. Jody and Carla would sneak drinks from the vodka miniatures Carla kept in her purse, and they would confide in each other, as girls did, I learned, in their quick and what seemed to me overly-quick-to-trust friendships.

Jody spoke of Carla, but I had not met her. I had supper at Denny's alone one night in order to see what kind of person she was, how she was with people. I felt I should know. She smiled a lot, that was the first thing—a toothy smile that revealed big, buck teeth. When she said, "What can I get you?" she spoke loudly enough to be heard tables away. When she turned you could see her breasts move under her pink uniform. The upper part of her body was large, but her legs were thin, and she darkened her small, pale eyes with makeup.

Halfway into December Jody and Carla Kirby happened to work the same shift and had an argument over who was going to wait on a certain man, a truck driver, who tipped well. He was put in Jody's section, Jody said, but Carla had come running over to say a big, loud hello, one arm going around his shoulder. Jody told me all this in detail. He said, "I'll have the BLT, honey, with fries," and Carla said to Jody, "Well, I might as well go ahead and get this," and Jody said, "Why should you? He's in my section," and Carla did anyway, and that was the end of their friendship. Jody said that Carla had cut the cord between them, and when Jody walked into the RV that afternoon she said, "I couldn't wait to get out of there. I just wanted to come home to you."

That meant a lot to me, and I wasn't sorry about the way it happened. I had not liked the bond they had formed; I don't think most men would have. But I didn't expect Jody to have so much difficulty losing her. Jody cried over it, said it reminded her of when a friend in middle school had moved to Nevada and never called or emailed. Just disappeared, Jody said. I didn't point out that it wasn't like that at all, that Carla hadn't disappeared, and that Jody could have let Carla wait on that trucker, and she and Carla could have remained friends. Why was it so important for Jody to wait on him, anyway? Just how much did that trucker mean to her? But I didn't want to be critical, especially when Jody seemed lost over the end of the friendship—not just lost but distraught, as in overly so. I tried to think of what might distract her.

"Let's go to the Humane Society and get a dog," I said. This was close to Christmas.

Jody had had one as a child, and I had had one as well, and naturally I liked the idea of Jody and me adopting one together.

"Really?" Jody said. "That would be all right with you?"

It was a chilly, gray afternoon, and as we drove there we discussed whether to choose a small dog or a large one, a male or female, and so on, and we came up with a list of names. But once we were at the shelter Jody got a glimpse of the dogs in cages, looking at us as their one hope, she said, their only way out, and she couldn't bring herself to choose one and leave the rest behind. It seemed unfair, she said. It seemed unfeeling.

In the parking lot she said, "Let's get as far from here as we can," and we drove into the mountains, all the way down to Kirkland and west to Bagdad, where snow started falling—big flakes as if the sky were weeping big tears, Jody said. I drove carefully, with Jody sitting close to me. She wouldn't wear a seat belt. It didn't matter how many times you asked her to. She gave a reason: in such-and-such a place somebody was killed in an accident because they were trapped in a seat belt. I told her it probably happened one time out of a hundred thousand, but she said no, it had to have happened a lot more than that, or else she wouldn't have heard of it. Anyway, she didn't want to wear one, and I couldn't make her, but I liked her sitting close; in that respect I didn't mind.

In Bagdad we pulled into the parking lot of the Mountain Tavern and stood in the snow, feeling it on our faces, opening our mouths and tasting it. Then we went inside and drank until we were warm and drunk, and we danced to Willie Nelson on the jukebox, even though I didn't know how to dance. But when you wanted something badly enough, you didn't have to know how. That was how love came into existence. Maybe that was how every important thing did.

I JUST WANTED to come home to you. I couldn't forget her saying that—the words, her voice, her expression. To me it proved that she knew she had a home with me. She could have driven home to me every night of her life, and I mean even if she never slept with me. Looking back, I believe I would have accepted that, if I had had to. I like to think I would have. Nobody understands that about men, about some men, and I don't mean men who don't care about sex because all men care about it and want it and fantasize about it. I mean men like me, who wouldn't settle for a girl other people might think was a more realistic choice—a girl not so pretty, a girl who saw the world as you did, a girl who wanted you. Granted, there weren't a lot of those around for me. Nonetheless I was aware of what I was choosing.

There was a day in my childhood when Lee and Sandra took me to the playground and I climbed up the big slide and saw them below me, Lee to the left and Sandra to the right, and I thought about jumping. Maybe I was trying to bring them together, not that I could have known that at the time; maybe I wanted to get away from them. Maybe I was having that impulse to jump that a lot of people have. Or maybe it was a thought that meant nothing at all except, wow, jumping was one of the possibilities that existed for you at the top of a slide.

But everything changed when I had that thought, when I saw that you could do something weird, something crazy, something nobody else would understand. That had to be true for everybody, I thought. It was a mistake to think that you weren't like other people. Nobody was special. Nobody was any more or less entitled to love the wrong person than I was.

chapter seventeen

TRAVIS ASPENALL

"J ODY WAS UNDER the bed, Travis. She was dead but she was moving her hands."

I turned on the light so that he could see me checking. Damien wouldn't take your word for anything.

"A pair of socks are under there," I said, "but that's it, and they're not moving."

He had his head over the side of the bed, making sure.

"We didn't know her," I said. "Don't think we did, Damien. We saw her once, when she was alive, but that was all."

"But we saw her dead."

"Doesn't count," I said.

From the hallway we heard Pete coming down the hall, back into the room with us. Now that he was older he slept on the braided rug between our beds. He couldn't jump onto Damien's bed anymore.

"There's Pete," Damien whispered, and I went back to bed and heard Damien's breathing slow down and mine slow down with it. I knew from science class that we were all physiologically affected by each other. Yawning was contagious; nobody knew why. And when girls hung out with each other, they got their periods at the same time. Placebos were another example. If you believed something was working, your body could respond as if it were working.

Then there was genetics—not just blue eyes or brown eyes but tendencies to be a certain kind of person: good, bad, kind, evil, whatever, if there were such a thing as evil. There was research done on twins who had not grown up together. There was a lot to discover, still. Similarities in brain chemistry lead to similar personalities, similar likes and dislikes. Then there were studies done on the differences between the genders—what was inborn and what was learned. In what ways did our brain chemistries differ? How much choice was involved in what we felt and thought? Why were we so different from each other?

I heard my parents getting ready for bed and the wind rise outside. In the spring the wind blew down hard at night from the Bradshaws. I looked at the shadows on the wall and thought about the five-sided house Harmony lived in on Wanda Drive. I had ridden my bike past often enough to know which room was hers. I had seen her through the window, in front of the mirror, brushing her hair, and I had hung around on my bike longer than I should have, given how bad it would have looked to her parents if they had seen me. I rode my bike around and around the block almost until dark, so that watching her was like watching a movie. She was sitting on her bed by then, with her iPod in her lap. I was hoping she would change her clothes, while I was watching, take off her top and change into a sweater. It was getting cold out by then. Instead her mother came to the doorway, and Harmony followed her out of the room and the movie was over.

I had done things with girls, not as much as Billy had, but probably more than Harmony knew. In the fifth and sixth grade girls used to call me. I hardly knew why, at first. That aspect of my life was easier than I had thought it would be. The girls I ended up doing things with were more into me than I was into them. I wouldn't think about it much, after. Then they'd be mad; I wasn't paying enough attention to them, and I would feel like a jerk for a while until the next girl came along. I didn't feel good about that, but I didn't feel as bad as somebody else might have. Now there was Harmony, and I wasn't on such safe ground.

"Travis," Damien said in his sleep. "I lost my shoe in the circus tent. Tell Dad to come build a bridge."

I heard a sound from outside that wasn't the wind, and I went into the kitchen and looked out the window and saw that Nate was on the patio with a screwdriver in his hand, tightening the bolts on my mother's glider. She had mentioned it once. Nate was in jeans and boots, without his shirt on. I hadn't realized how skinny he was, how much weight he had lost in the little bit of time he had been here, or maybe before that. We hadn't seen him in some time. He hadn't wanted us to visit, and now we knew that it was because Jody Farnell had moved in with him. He had told my father that. She had been living in a motel, when we met her. He didn't say why he hadn't wanted us to know. Just that she had been sharing his RV, and then she had moved to Winslow, where she was from.

Nate sat in the glider, pushing himself back and forth on it with his foot. Then he was on his hands and knees with WD-40, oiling the springs. Next he stood on a chair and straightened out my mother's wind chime, which had tangled in the wind, and after that I watched him put the WD-40 on the patio table, next to the pliers, and then slowly and carefully climb to the top of the ridge behind our house. He stood with his arms out to either side as if they were the wings of a hawk. The sky was starry and the moon was above him. Then he put his arms down and looked in the direction of the wash where we had found Jody. You could see a long way, from where he was, all the way to where we had found her. He looked for a long time, as if he could see her.

Then he climbed down from the ridge and stood in the clearing between our house and the Airstream. His arms were hanging loose at his sides. His head was bent down. I thought about going out there to let him know somebody was watching. It seemed so private, what he was doing, even though he wasn't doing anything. But he was heading to the Airstream with slow steps. He went inside and closed the door.

chapter eighteen

SAM RUSH

JODY FARNELL'S 2001 Corolla was discovered on Bucket of Blood Drive in Holbrook, which was thirty miles east of Winslow. The Navajo County deputy sheriff who called me with the information said, "Odd, isn't it? The car left on that particular road? Makes you think it had to be intentional."

He had found the car himself, he told me, pretty much by accident. The Toyota was undamaged, with the license plate removed. In the back seat was a red sweater, a small pillow, a brown microfiber blanket, and a brochure from La Posada hotel in Winslow. What appeared to be a small, hand-drawn map, in pencil, without street names, was in the compartment between the front seats. A destination on the map was marked with a small, hard-to-make-out symbol. In the glove compartment was the Toyota manual, and under the driver's seat, crumpled, was a cash receipt for a night's stay, the night of April 23, at the Old Route 66 Western Motel, in Flagstaff. And that was it. No blood, no signs of a struggle, no fingerprints, no cell phone, no purse, no journal.

"You'd expect to find the victim's fingerprints, obviously," said the deputy sheriff. "But they were only on her belongings. The car itself was wiped down well, whoever did it. I mean inside and out. Yet that receipt and the map were left there."

He faxed me the receipt and the map and told me that a woman named Paulette Hebson, who owned Hebson's Automobile Graveyard, just to the south of Bucket of Blood Drive, could show me the specific location. He had spoken with her. I drove to Holbrook and met with her. She was a stocky, attractive, blonde woman in her late fifties. Polly, she said to call her. She wore men's clothes—jeans and a Carhartt jacket.

Her house and office were just south of the automobile graveyard, and in the strong, midafternoon sun she walked me north across the property. It was a shining jumble of cars and pickups and semi cabs and farming equipment, bordered on the north by Bucket of Blood Drive, where the car was found. The deputy sheriff had come upon the Toyota on his way to her junkyard with his son, who was looking for a carburetor. Paulette herself had not noticed the Toyota, but then, as I had just seen, she said, she lived to the south. She didn't usually drive down that particular stretch of the road.

"I don't know how long it would have taken me to notice it myself," she said. "And if I had, I probably wouldn't have thought anything about it."

"Were you aware of Jody Farnell's death?"

"I read about it in the paper," she said. "It was sad, how young she was. But she was from Winslow, and the body was found a long way from there, if I'm remembering right. Somewhere in the direction of Phoenix? And of course I'd never heard of her. So I doubt if I would have connected it."

"Do you recall seeing anybody around in the last few weeks, anybody or anything that might have made you wonder for just a second?"

She stood a minute, thinking, with her back to the sun. The wind blew her hair back from her face.

"I don't recall anything unusual," she said. "But I'm inside doing paperwork a good deal of the time." She smiled. "That's what nobody tells you about running a business. The paperwork."

"What about whoever works for you? Might they have seen anything?"

"Women run things alone these days, Deputy Sheriff. At least this woman does. There's just me here. I followed in my father's footsteps. He was the one who started the business, and when he died I took over."

"That was some time ago?"

"Seventeen years."

"So you've never hired anybody to help you?" I said, "even briefly?"

"I never needed help."

"You have any family that helps out? A sibling, or one of your kids? Anybody who knows this place fairly well?"

"No," she said. "I had a brother who died in Vietnam, but that was it. No husband, no child. No children."

I nodded and looked at the street sign.

"Bucket of Blood Drive," I said. "It's an odd name for a street. Do you know where it comes from?"

"Everybody does. There used to be an old saloon along it, a wild place, apparently. In the 1800s there was a gunfight there, which left what was said to be buckets of blood on the floor. So that became the name of the place. If you drive down a few blocks, you can see the stone walls that are left. There's a plaque put up. Anyway, Holbrook used to be a rough, cowboy town, and that street used to be called Central, but for the sake of history, and a good story, I suppose, it got changed."

"You wonder if whoever left Jody Farnell's car here," I said, "liked the idea of being thought of as rough and tough, like those outlaw cowboys back then. You know anybody like that? Does anybody at all come to mind?"

"My grandfather, dead now." She smiled again. "But no. I don't know of anybody like that. I don't know of anyone who would have hurt a woman."

We walked back through the automobile graveyard. Beyond it to the south was mostly empty desert sloping down to the wash of the Little Colorado River. I wondered why somebody would have gone all the way to Black Canyon City to deposit Jody's body in a wash that wasn't substantially different from this one, if you left out the view of the mountains and the fact that the Aspenalls lived near it. Unless Jody had left the car here herself, for some reason I couldn't imagine, before getting into another vehicle, or unless the car had been stolen and abandoned here, which seemed unlikely. It was in good condition for a relatively old car, but it was old enough not to be a temptation.

I GOT ONTO I-40 and got off in Winslow, stopping at the drive-up window of Burger King for coffee, then sitting in my SUV, looking at my fax of the map found in Jody's car. I phoned Alice Weneka, the woman who had taken in Wes Giddens, and asked if we could talk in person. My intention was twofold: to question her about Wes Giddens, and to see if she, being Navajo, recognized the symbol on the map as Navajo. It looked possibly Native American to me.

She lived on North Prairie in a white stucco house with a red-tiled roof and wooden shutters, and she came to the door with a small boy in her arms—her younger daughter's child, she said. He had a cold. She invited me in and offered me coffee, and in the sunlit kitchen she held her grandson on her lap. She was a small woman with deep brown eyes and less gray in her hair than I had.

"It must be hard not to have Hannah nearby," I said. "You ever wonder why Wes doesn't bring her home to see you, from wherever he is? Just for a visit?"

"Well, he's probably in college by now, and has a new life. That was what he wanted for himself."

"You don't keep in touch by phone, then," I said.

"I'm not much for the telephone."

"Seems strange to me, though, that he wouldn't want to tell you about Hannah, how she's doing and so forth."

She resettled her restless grandson. "Between my two daughters I have five grandchildren, and they all live near here," she said. "I have enough, Deputy Sheriff."

"Can you show me the picture you have of Hannah?"

She went into the other room and came back with the same picture Jody's mother had shown me—a tiny three-month Hannah, lying on her back in a crib in a blue-walled room.

"Where was this taken?" I asked.

"My sister's house," Alice said.

"Here in Winslow?"

"On the Reservation."

"As I mentioned on the phone," I said, "Jody Farnell told a lot of people that she wanted to get Hannah back from Wes. That she wanted to find out where Wes and Hannah were and so on. Jody never contacted you about that? Not even after she moved back to Winslow?"

"No," Alice said. "I didn't know she had moved back."

"I thought everybody here in Winslow knew everybody else, or at least everybody else's business."

"My community is mostly family, Deputy Sheriff, and Navajo. And while we thought of Wes as family, well, Jody wasn't known to us. That's how I would put it."

"But you knew her."

"A little."

"How much is that?" I said.

"I saw her twice. Perhaps three times at most. Long ago."

She let her grandson off her lap and he stood uncertainly, one hand on her knee.

"He's just started to walk," Alice explained.

"He has a lot to experience then."

"Yes."

"While I'm here," I said, "I wonder if I could ask your help with something."

I showed her the map and told her where it had been found, and she put on her reading glasses and took her time studying it.

"What about the symbol?" I said. "I thought it might make sense to you from your Navajo religion."

"It's not a Navajo symbol, or Hopi or Apache, for that matter, not anything I'm familiar with. I don't know what it signifies."

"Does the configuration of roads look familiar to you?"

She looked at the map carefully. "No," she said. "It seems like it could be lots of places."

"Any of those places come to mind?"

"I didn't mean that," she said. "Just that it could be anywhere."

She took off her glasses and picked up the little boy, then she walked me to the door and told me to be careful driving. She had been to a funeral that morning, she said. Her cousin's wife, Ida, had been killed. "Just driving into Winslow for groceries, you know, like she does every week. Expecting to get there and home safe."

"We all have that expectation, don't we?" I said, and she nodded, holding her grandson on her hip. As I left, he lifted his hand in a wave.

Outside, the wind was cool and the sun low. On the wide streets of Winslow people were driving home from work past empty storefronts in the small town that had once been the second largest in northern Arizona. I drove to La Posada, a restored railroad hotel, and spoke to a young man at the front desk in the lobby, which doubled as a shop selling Native American jewelry. I showed the man photographs of Nate Aspenall and Jody Farnell, and he said, "I don't recognize them, but I'm just part-time here. Let me keep a copy and I'll ask."

From Winslow I drove to Flagstaff and located the Old Route 66 Western Motel and spoke to the clerk at the front desk. On the night in question, they had had eight single-room occupants, among them a Nate Aspenall from Chino Valley, with a 2003 blue Ford F150.

I was disheartened on behalf of the Aspenalls, but I wasn't surprised. As much as Nate had cared for Jody, as hard as he had tried to remain close to her, it had seemed inconceivable to me that he wouldn't have gone to see her more than the one time he had met her in Flagstaff. As for why he had lied, well, people lied not just for the obvious reasons, but for reasons that never made sense to anybody else. They lied to you, or they lied to everybody but you, or they lied to themselves—you came to expect the unpredictability of it and lack of apparent meaning. So I didn't waste time speculating. I did wonder why Nate would have left that receipt in Jody's car, but in a rush and in an anxious state, he might have simply missed seeing it.

I ARRIVED IN Black Canyon City in time for a late supper at the Rock Springs Café, where Audrey Birdsong had the night off, it turned out. That was my second disappointment of the day, and for the moment this one mattered more to me. I hadn't realized how much I had looked forward to seeing her until I walked in to find her not there.

The following morning, first thing, I phoned Lee and told him that Nate had been in Flagstaff, just fifty miles from Winslow, the night before Jody was killed. "He needs to come forward with that information, on his own. It's the smartest thing he can do. Maybe you can get through to him."

chapter nineteen

NATE ASPENALL

JODY'S MOTHER WAS calling with problems. This began late in December. A boyfriend had stolen money from the mother, rats had gotten into her trailer, the "bitchy" woman next door had called the police because the mother's music was too loud, the mother had sprained her foot, and there was nobody to take care of her. Wasn't Jody the only person her mother could trust? Shouldn't Jody look after her mother just as her mother had looked after Jody all those years of growing up?

Jody would go outside after the calls. She would sit on the steps of the RV with a blanket around her shoulders and her hands in her lap, one nestled in the other.

"Come inside," I would tell her, and she would say okay and wouldn't move. Her mother turned her into a stone, a statue. I couldn't stand how remote she became. Out of desperation one night I said, "Come inside, honey," and when she turned to me I saw the power it held for a girl. She came in from the cold and sat beside me. She said, "Make me a drink, Nate," and I did.

The following night I had the thought that she would have sex with me if I said, "Sleep with me, honey." I know how cold that makes me sound. But I believed it would be good for her to make love with a man she could depend on. That would be a change for her. She and I were watching television, when I was considering this; we were sitting on the futon together, and I turned to her to say it. But before I could, she looked at me as if she were seeing somebody else—Wes Giddens, perhaps, or one of the men from the restaurant, somebody who had ended up letting her down. Or else it was Nate Aspenall she was seeing, and I was seeing in her face that none of her wanted me.

"I'm going for a walk," I said. Quickly, I put on my jacket and left before I had a chance to say or do something that revealed the humiliation I felt, the anger, the confusion, the distance between my intention and her reaction. I almost lost track of the fact that I had not said what I had planned and she had not rejected me. Not this time.

It was after eleven, dark and cold. The moon was a sharp, white sliver, and lining the roads of the park was the frozen, dirty last of a snowfall. I walked fast, trying to exhaust myself past feeling. But before long I had in my mind a story Jody had told me about a party she had gone to in high school, a drunken party at which kids disappeared with each other into bedrooms to experiment with sex—not intercourse, Jody said, not for her, not except once, she said, along with some "other things," which she did not name, that she had not done before.

"The world is different from when you were young, Nate," she said, and I had wanted to say, bring me up to date, then, Jody. Show me how the world works now. I couldn't see why engaging in sex with people she hardly knew was all right but I wasn't. I couldn't see what it would have cost her.

The wind was gusting and the air was crystallized and haloed under the old-fashioned light posts we had in the RV park. In a few RVs I heard televisions going and saw the glow of them through the curtains. But most people were asleep; many of the residents were middle-aged and older. I started seeing myself in the future, lonely and old, having never had a wife or a family or what Lee and Sandra would have called a real job, a real house, a real life. I knew that what they expected of me I had not accomplished and probably never would. I was a loser, of sorts; that was how they saw me and probably how Jody saw me. But she was in that same category herself, it seemed to me, if not in a worse one. That was what was in my head that night.

Sandra took me to a psychologist when I was in the sixth grade. The school counselor had suggested it. He has a high IQ, but low grades, Sandra was told. He doesn't speak in class or make friends. The psychologist's office was in a brick building near the hospital, with a courtyard. I resented the psychologist's personal questions, not that I answered them. No and yes were all I said.

Afterward Sandra and I went to supper at a Mexican restaurant near Prescott College. I told Sandra I didn't want to see the psychologist again, and she said, "Are you sure, Nate?" But I could see she was relieved; it had cost so much. She said, "Use your intelligence in your own way. And talk to people sometimes." Later, she would call Lee, and they would buy me a computer and ask if I wanted to be on a soccer team or join the Boy Scouts.

At supper she was cheery, drinking a margarita. She was always that way at first, then she would get an abandoned look afterward. Whenever we went out, people recognized her from the billboards that advertized the dealership she worked for, and sometimes a man would come up to us. "You don't know me," she would say. "What sense does this make?" It bothered her that they would ask her out in front of me, and it bothered me as well. I didn't like thinking about her with men. This was before Ernest Sterling, the only one of her boyfriends to live with us, and the only one I liked.

Saturday nights Sandra and I sat on her bed, with chips and salsa, watching movies. Above us was a yellow and orange Indian bedspread tacked to the ceiling. She had put a blue and green one on the ceiling in my room. Our house on Delia Lane, off Nightfall, was small: two bedrooms, a bathroom, a tiny kitchen, a narrow living room Sandra and I painted orange. A creek ran behind the house, and in the backyard were two cottonwoods and a willow. We put up a tent and slept there, some nights. Our neighbors were students, mostly, and when they felt like it they came over and had a beer with Sandra and played computer games with me.

I spent every other weekend with Lee. He had moved to Black Canyon City by then and lived in a duplex on Abbott Street, next door to Sam Rush. I remember a girlfriend he had one year who accidentally slammed Sam's cat in a door. I remember a blue bicycle Lee bought me, and he and Sam teaching me to ride it. Lee had quit drinking by then, and was quieter, not all over the place anymore, tossing a ball, breaking a window, wanting to take me to this place or that place.

I'd feel him watching me, trying to figure out who I was now that he was sober and he could see me. I believe he did feel love for me, but he was seventeen when I was born. I was a baby doll somebody handed him. A bag of flour like we had had to cart around in our ninth-grade health class. It's a baby, they told us. You can't leave it. It can't survive without you.

I'd see the look on Sandra's face when Lee picked me up, every other Friday afternoon. She would stand in the yard, watching me go, and I would make myself wave to her until Lee turned the corner and she couldn't see me anymore. That was the price I had to pay. When he brought me home, Sundays, she wouldn't talk to me or look at me, at first, then she would give me a tight hug, hold me too long, ask too many questions.

As I got older and stayed in my room, reading, Sandra would say, "Why don't you want to be with me anymore?" and I would say, "Because I'm a teenager now. That's what teenagers do." She seemed not to know how that worked. We weren't in sync during those years, but it wasn't like we didn't eat supper together or talk some. It was true that I never called her Mom, or Lee Dad, but that meant nothing. I had always called them what they called each other, but it wasn't like I didn't know who they were to me.

Delia Lane comes into my dreams even now—the small, low houses; the empty field at the end of the street; the black pickup that ran over my dog when I was seven. I dream of storm clouds hovering over the creek; of a house next door that is just like our house except the windows and doors are boarded up. What happened there? I want to know. In my dreams I'm always asking.

THAT NIGHT IN Chino Valley I was so cold I was numb when I got back. Behind the partition Jody was asleep, oblivious. There was relief in that. When I was a small kid I thought people could read your mind. I thought you had to monitor the inside of your head, keep right thoughts on display and wrong thoughts hidden. I felt that pressure all the time.

When I woke the following morning it was late. Jody had gone to work and left me a note: *You have a fever. I felt your forehead.* She had put her hand on me; that was what struck me. I looked at the note for a long time—the large loops of her letters, the smiley face with which she dotted the *I*. The night before seemed a long time ago. I had a hard time remembering how the whole thing had started.

chapter twenty

TRAVIS ASPENALL

"IN ORDER TO anticipate what might happen, Travis," Dad said, "in any situation, you have to train yourself to see things the way other people might. Do you understand what I'm saying?"

It was Saturday, and my father had gotten me up early. Before Nate had started working at the veterinary clinic, it had been my job, Saturday mornings, to clean the animals' cages and mop the floors in the examining rooms. "We don't want Travis to lose his work ethic," Dad had said to Mom at breakfast. "Before long Nate will go home, and Travis will have to get used to working again."

Once Dad and I were on our way he wasn't in a hurry to get there. He pulled into the Roadrunner in New River and ordered coffee. We sat at a table outside in the chilly morning, with the sun spilling across the desert. The air was so clear that you could see as far as the foothills of Carefree, and Dad looked at the landscape, and that was when he started talking.

"It seems as if Nate might have gone up to see Jody before she died," he said. "There's no crime in that, and it's easy to understand why he might not have told Sam Rush. Nobody wants to be suspected of doing what he didn't do, Travis, and nobody wants to admit to chasing after a girl. Nate does have an alibi, of a sort. He was home in Chino Valley that night. But his neighbors can't verify having seen him or his pickup."

Dad paused when the coffee arrived. I had ordered a Coke.

"So the possibility of Nate having gone to see Jody when he did," he said, "is just between us. You're old enough to understand the importance of that."

"You mean don't tell Nate we know," I said.

"It's simplest to say nothing to anybody. That's the best thing. It's what is required of you as a man, and here's what I mean by that. In a family it's the husband and father who's responsible for more than the family realizes. The family has to be able to depend on him, no matter what. In my opinion that's how it should be. It doesn't mean that Mom isn't responsible, or that she's less important than I am. It just means that I know what I need to do in order for my family to be able to count on me, whether she or anybody else realizes it."

"So Mom doesn't know what you're telling me," I said.

Dad glanced at the door opening and two men in work clothes coming outside.

He said, "No. Not yet. Mom and I are in this together, Travis, but until Nate was in college she didn't know him. She didn't see firsthand what Nate had to deal with, between Sandra and me. Nate didn't get to have the kind of childhood you and Damien have had."

"I know that."

"And Mom knows it, too. But she didn't see it. Nate might be something of a mystery to her. There's no way she can understand him the way I can. What you can't understand, you can misunderstand. Do you see what I'm saying?"

He stopped to drink his coffee.

"I realize that I'm putting a lot on you," he said. "Normally I would have Sam to talk to, but, well, you see the situation."

"Sam doesn't trust Nate, you mean."

Dad took off his windbreaker. The day was heating up.

"You could say that it's Sam's job not to trust Nate," he said. "And here's what he's faced with. Nate is the only person connecting Jody Farnell to where her body was found. That's how things stand, Travis, even though that in itself makes it unlikely Nate had anything to do with this—the obviousness, I mean. Why would Nate do that to himself?"

The waitress came outside and poured Dad more coffee. I waited until she had gone.

"What if Nate went to see Jody and he killed her without meaning to?"

Dad's eyes were on the desert.

"If that's what happened," he said, "then that's what happened, and we'll support Nate however we can." Dad knocked the table with his knuckles, as he did whenever he was making a point about something.

He took out his wallet and left money on the table. But after we got in the Jeep he didn't move for a minute.

"Nate used to do this thing on the phone," he said. "He must have been seven or eight or so. He would say, 'Is this the party with whom I'm speaking?' I suppose he heard it on television. He was always smarter than people gave him credit for."

Then Dad started the Jeep and we drove to his clinic. Cave Creek was made up of a collection of small businesses straggled along Cave

Creek Road, and the clinic was at the northwestern end. Inside I got the dogs from the cages in the back—a collie mix and two who-knew-whats—and took them out to the fenced-in area behind the clinic, from where you could see the small houses along the side street. For a brief while Dad came out and stood with me. It was still early enough that the birds were noisy. The collie mix started digging a hole under the fence, and Dad said, "She wants out, and who can blame her?" He whistled and reached into his pocket for the treats he carried.

WE LEFT THE clinic early in the afternoon, stopped for hamburgers, and discovered at home that my mother, Damien, and Nate were taking down the curtains in the house.

"Spring cleaning," Dad said. "She goes crazy every year." But he joined in, and so did I; we didn't have a choice. We worked until five, when Dad and Nate went to pick up Chinese food, which we ate outside as the sun went down.

"Where's Pete?" Nate said.

None of us knew. We looked in the house and around the house, then went out to Canyon Road and up to the ridge. He wasn't anywhere, and it was getting dark. We sat on the patio, hoping to see him emerge from somewhere in the dusk.

"He'll come back when he's ready," Dad said, but we knew it had been years since he had gone off like that. Meanwhile five mule deer were filing down from the ridge to drink from the small, shallow pool Dad and I had dug under the palo verde tree. They walked as silently as Indians, or at least as silently as Indians walked in movies. Harmony, I thought, probably hated those movies. She probably saw all kinds of things differently from the way I did.

One by one the deer filed up to the ridge.

"The javelina will be next," Dad said.

Ten minutes passed. Then six of them emerged in a clumsy group from the desert beyond the Airstream. Mom went inside for the carrots she tossed them, which they ate noisily.

"They're such pigs," Dad said.

Nate walked a few feet away from us and looked at Venus, which was low and bright over the ridge. But I knew it was Pete he was looking and listening for. We all were.

Eight months ago, at daybreak, Nate had been with us when we had taken the ashes of Pete's sister, Bodie, up to the ridge, opened the tin box, and watched the wind distribute them. "She's not in the pain of the world anymore," Mom had said.

Three hours later, after we had all gone to bed, I heard the sound of Pete's bark and found him standing outside the kitchen door. Good things could happen, but not always, I thought, and not forever.

chapter twenty-one

SAM RUSH

T HE WOMAN AT La Posada told me on the phone that she recognized the couple in the photocopies. She had sold them a ring. The girl had tried on six or seven, the woman said. She was drawn to them.

"They didn't have much," the woman said. "You could see that, and the boyfriend—well, I assumed he was her boyfriend—offered to buy her one. You could see she didn't expect that. He told her, 'It's worth it to me,' and in the end they bought a ring with a slender, curved coral stone, an inch and a half in length, outlined in tooled silver. I can fax you a picture of it. We keep photographs of all our jewelry.

"The boyfriend paid cash for it, and the girl didn't want a box. She wore the ring on her index finger, I believe it was. She had small hands, small fingers. And if I'm not mistaken it was her left hand she put it on. I recall thinking, well, that relationship will never work. The girl looked unhappy, and you got the impression the man wanted to fix that. So of course it was unworkable."

"Anything else you recall either of them saying?"

"I believe the girl said something like, 'I'll wear it all the time. I won't take it off.' Then they talked about where they might go for a drink. I figured, with how little they had, they'd go somewhere like PT's, which is not far from here. Well, nothing's far in Winslow. Or perhaps the girl mentioned PT's. I can't be certain. In any case they went into the bar here at La Posada, and as I was leaving work later I saw them come out to the parking lot and get into a small, orange car. I recall thinking how glad I was, never having to be their age again."

Two hours later Nate called my cell and said he had something to tell me. He asked me to meet him at the Satisfied Frog, on Cave Creek Road. He was already in Cave Creek, he said. He was at his father's veterinary clinic. He could walk to the restaurant from there.

When I arrived he was sitting at a quiet booth in the back. He wore a gray sweatshirt, and his hair hung straight and limp in his eyes. He had ordered a beer for himself, and there was a Coke on the table for me. He started talking as soon as I sat down.

"I went to Winslow to see Jody the day before she was killed," he said. "I spent the afternoon with her, then at six or so I left, and stopped in Flagstaff for the night."

"At the Old Route 66 Western Motel."

"So you know that," he said.

"Yes."

"How?"

"The motel receipt was found under the driver's seat of Jody's car."

"Her car was found?" he said. "Where?"

If he knew the answer, he was doing a good job seeming not to.

"How do you suppose your receipt got into her car?" I said.

"We went to La Posada in her car," he said. "I must have dropped it somehow."

"You hadn't stayed there yet," I said.

His eyes darted away from mine to the basket of unshelled peanuts that were on the table.

"I don't know how then," he said. "I can't imagine. I got confused."

"It's an important point," I said.

He was silent. He took a nervous drink of his beer.

"We'll come back to that," I told him. "So you went to Winslow and got there in the afternoon."

Nate touched the basket of peanuts.

"She was calling me late at night," he said, "saying she had made a bad mistake. Saying that one thing again and again."

"The mistake was what?"

"Moving back to Winslow. Everything had gone wrong, she said. Her mother didn't need her except to use her. Wes Giddens wasn't living anywhere near there, not that she could find out, which meant that Hannah was further away than she had thought, further away than she could get to. Everybody wanted things, Jody said. She should have known that about people, she said, and now she did. I was the only one who didn't want anything from her. That was why she was calling me. Just to hear my voice, she said."

"Then what?" I said.

"On this particular night she said she was sorry for calling, that it was selfish of her, and she hung up. She had called from a bar called PT's, and it was late, and I tried to go back to sleep. But it wasn't like Jody to apologize straight out like that, and her voice was strange. She sounded hopeless. In the morning I set out for Winslow, and when I got there she had just come home."

"What time was this?"

"I don't know," he said. "Three in the afternoon or so. She said let's go somewhere, and she told me about La Posada, and we got into her car and that was where we went."

"You didn't go into her house?"

"She didn't want me to."

"Why not? Did she say?"

"No." Nate was chewing on a fingernail. "You're probably thinking somebody might have been watching. Some man she knew."

"Is that how it seemed to you?"

"I don't know," Nate said. "I don't know how it seemed. Maybe she didn't want me to see how she was living. She had dreams for herself, you know, like getting Hannah back, and maybe she didn't want to see her life as I might have, as it really was. You know what I mean? It's possible."

"So the two of you went to La Posada. I know that you bought her a ring there. Tell me about that."

He looked up at me, his eyes so dark they seemed opaque.

"I was going to tell you about the ring," he said, "even though I don't see that it's important except to me."

"So tell me now," I said.

He looked at the waitress coming toward us and asked her for another beer. He was polite and quiet-spoken, as he always was, and didn't make eye contact with her, nor did he watch her as she walked away.

"They sell Indian jewelry in the lobby. They had three or four boxes of rings, most of them old, and Jody was pulled in their direction. They weren't as expensive as I was afraid they would be, and I told her I would buy her one. It wasn't like she expected me to. She tried a lot of them on. She had a hard time making up her mind. Then she chose one and said it made her feel hopeful, like there was good luck in it. She said she would never take it off. I figured she had it on when Travis and Damien found her."

"You and Jody went into the bar at La Posada," I said. "I know that. What did the two of you talk about?"

"Chino Valley," he said quietly. "We talked about the small deck she wanted me to build onto the RV. She used to suggest that a lot. We talked about a Chinese restaurant we used to keep hearing about. I guess we talked about things we almost but never did. Then I . . ."

"What?"

When he spoke I could scarcely hear him.

"I asked her to marry me. She said, 'You want to marry me, even though we never . . .' And I said yes. She asked if she could think about it for a while, and I said sure."

"And after that?" I said.

"She wanted to go for a drive as the sun went down. We went on the Reservation and drove to a town called Leupp and back. That was her idea."

"Why there? There was something or somebody there she wanted to see?"

"I don't think so. There aren't many roads around there, at least not paved ones. Maybe it was one of the few she knew."

"What about after the drive?"

"She said she had to cook supper for her mother. 'You go back to Chino Valley,' she said. Meanwhile she would think about what I had asked her."

The waitress brought Nate his beer without his noticing.

"But you only went as far as Flagstaff," I said.

"I wanted to spend the night at a motel in Winslow. Any motel. But she said no, that she needed more time. She needed to make sure that if she said yes, she was saying it for the right reason. That was what she told me, that she didn't want to use me. So I left."

"For Flagstaff."

"I didn't tell her that. I let her think I was going home—doing what she wanted me to."

"So why didn't you?"

Nate put his hands flat on the table. He had thin hands and long fingers, like his father.

"I just didn't. It didn't feel right."

"You went straight to Flagstaff?"

"I stopped for pizza, then I went to the motel."

"And in the morning?"

"I filled up my truck, got a biscuit from McDonald's, and drove home."

"I don't know, Nate," I said. "It doesn't make much sense to me, your staying in Flagstaff, but not returning to Winslow in the morning. They're not but forty-five minutes apart. In fact if it were me," I said, "I would have wondered what difference it would have made to Jody, your staying overnight in Winslow, as you had wanted to. It's a long drive from there to Chino Valley, and it was already dusk. Had you driven home, you would have had to make that long round trip in one day."

"Maybe she figured I would stay the night somewhere."

"Then why say no to your staying in Winslow?" I said. "Did you wonder?"

"She wanted time to think. Time and space."

"But you had some idea of other men in her life," I said. "You must have had some suspicion as to why she wanted you out of town so fast. It would have been natural to drive back there late that night, perhaps, or the next day, to see what you could see. That would be understandable. I imagine the two of you had a talk in her car, which was how the receipt ended up there. That's what makes sense to me. So let's make this easy, Nate. Just tell me the sequence of events."

"I didn't go back."

"Make that believable to me."

"I was afraid she'd turn down my proposal if I did that."

"Maybe she did say no. Is that what happened, Nate? She called you the next day and told you no? Or you showed up in Winslow the following day and she told you no? It's a hard thing to be turned down, when you have already put up with so much. I can see how that would feel."

"Don't talk to me like a detective," Nate said. "I asked you to meet me so that I could tell you what I know, and I'm telling you."

"All right. I appreciate that. I'm asking you to do more of it, Nate. It's in your best interest."

"What would you think if I told you I went back the next day?"

"That you're human," I said. "That it's understandable. And it would explain how your motel receipt got in her car."

"And that I killed her."

"Not necessarily."

"I've told you from the beginning that I didn't hurt Jody," he said. "What you want me to do is defend myself as if I did."

"What choice do you have?" I said.

Nate's expression turned blankly dull. He didn't answer. His beer remained untouched in front of him.

chapter twenty-two

NATE ASPENALL

IT WAS AROUND New Year's that Jody began talking about Winslow. I don't mean a detail or story or two, but always. It was the only thing on her mind. It was like she was following a map inside herself, like an internal GPS system, like a migrating pattern that had brought her to Chino Valley and would take her home again in the spring. I was divided between fearing it and observing it. There was something compelling about seeing somebody getting ready to do something self-destructive. It was like watching a person walk into a fire. You wanted to shout no, but knew it wouldn't stop them. I suppose that was the worst part. They weren't going to listen. You didn't matter enough to them. Let them go, a part of you says. Let them walk into the flames and see that you were right.

At the same time I dreaded that she would leave without telling me, that I would come home one afternoon and she would be gone. I became so afraid that I started spying on her when she came home from working the lunch shift. I would stand behind the RV as she went in to change out of her uniform, then I would watch her come out to fill the bird feeder, which was too high for her to reach without standing tiptoe. I would wait to see a bit of her pale back when her sweatshirt drew up.

I had come to believe that pretty girls got used to being watched by men, so used to it that they behaved as if they were being watched even when they were alone. I imagined that Jody knew I was watching, and that what we were doing was a silent form of communicating. But I was wrong. I came out from behind the RV one afternoon and startled her into tears. After that I pulled back and stayed away most afternoons. I had to talk myself into letting what was going to happen, happen. But it got increasingly harder to come back to the RV not knowing if her car would be there. I had to steel myself for that, each evening, talk myself into being a stronger person than I was. Weakness is a hard thing to acknowledge in yourself, and to some extent I blamed mine on her, whether or not she deserved it.

FOR JODY'S BIRTHDAY I took her to Jerome for lunch at the Jerome Tavern, which had been a brothel, long ago, when the mining company was in operation. It was a bright, cold Saturday. After lunch we walked down the steep, narrow streets, with Jody looking in the shops at the artwork and pottery. I bought her a silver wind chime, and she held my hand as we left the shop. She said, "Tomorrow let's put it in the euca-lyptus tree," and I put a lot of hope on that, more than I should have. Then there was the hand-holding, which was something she seldom did. It was a powerful thing, the touch of another person. Right away it goes to your heart, especially if you're not used to it. She had to know the effect it had.

But on the drive home she said, "It's snowing in Winslow. My mother sent me a text," and I saw that nothing in her plans had changed—those plans she had not acknowledged to me outright, and possibly not to herself.

She told me that she had woken up the night before with this idea that people should die where they had been born—that the end should be like the beginning. "That's morbid," I told her, and she said no, she didn't mean it that way.

"Where you're from and what happened to you there matters. It's important. It's your history, even the parts you're ashamed of. Do you see what I mean, Nate? How even the bad parts belong to you?"

"What kind of bad parts?" I asked her. "Are you talking about when you were using drugs?"

"How can you bring that up when I've already paid such a price for what I did?"

"You more or less brought it up," I told her.

"Did I?" she said.

When she grew silent and huddled against the passenger door I started to see that I had given my life and myself away. Maybe at one time or another everybody does. I understood that human beings were lost, that we handed ourselves over and didn't know how to get ourselves back. I had acquired this habit of observing what was going on with myself, seeing my mechanisms, my inner workings. I could separate myself and see what I was up to, even though I could never stop what I was doing. I couldn't learn. I could see, but I couldn't change. It was a dangerous way to be, I began to see, like looking into a mirror so long that you start not to recognize your reflection. You have to move your hand or leg, reassure yourself that your brain is telling your body what to do, that is, that they're connected. You have to feel yourself become just the one organism.

THAT NIGHT JODY and I lay together on the rug and watched *They Came from Outer Space*. Slowly Jody began to tell me about the Winslow boyfriend with whom she had moved to Chino Valley. She said that he was the one who had helped her stop using drugs because he had stopped, and that they hadn't loved each other but needed each other for that short time, to get away from Winslow, to find out who they would be in another place. He got a job as a bouncer at the Star Tavern, in Prescott Valley, and she danced there for two months. She used to have a picture of herself up on the stage, she said, and described it all to me: the red g-string, the high heels, the peace-symbol necklace she wore so that customers could see her wanting what was best for the world. She had liked men looking at her, she said, so long as she had the boyfriend there, but he fell in love with somebody shortly after that, another girl who danced, which was when Jody started renting a motel room by the month and waitressing at Denny's.

"Do you still have what you wore?" I asked her, and she said no. She said she was down on herself, one night, thinking about it, and she threw the underwear and shoes in a Dumpster. She kept the peace symbol. She thought it might help her make peace with herself someday. She hoped that was possible. Maybe hating yourself for your actions was an act against the universe or something, she said, for you were part of the universe, she believed, and the world was forgiving. Grass grew where you wouldn't think it could. Daffodils appeared after the coldest winters.

All that night I woke up with pictures in my head of Jody on that stage. I tried to focus instead on the other things she had said, but your mind does what it wants, late at night, in the quiet, and after all, she had paraded that in front of me. The next morning I went to the mall and bought a red thong for her and red high heels, and that evening I said, "Do you want a rum and Coke, Jody?" I made her one and one for myself, and I said, "Would you do something for me?"

It had begun to snow outside and she was sitting at the window, watching it settle on the trees. "Like what?" she said, and I showed her what I had bought her. I saw the disappointment and sorrow in her eyes. She had expected more from me.

"Never mind," I said. "That was a mistake on my part."

I turned on the television as if it had not happened. I practically convinced myself it hadn't. But the next morning she appeared in the kitchen wearing only the thong and high heels, and she danced a few steps.

"See?" she said. "This is how I looked up on that stage."

Then she put on her robe and made coffee.

chapter twenty-three

TRAVIS ASPENALL

H ARMONY SHOWED ME the grade she had gotten on her history paper. This was after third period. Her first D, she said. She was supposed to have chosen one of the twentieth-century wars to write about. Instead she had written about the fact that people who had never fought in a war, or seen one up close, were ignorant on the subject. Any account of a war that wasn't firsthand was not worth reading. There was nothing you could learn from it.

"I expected to get a C," she said, "and that would have been all right with me. It's true that I didn't do what I was supposed to do. But a D isn't fair. I spent a lot of time on the paper, and I felt I had important things to say."

She was upset, and I had to stop myself from saying, It doesn't matter what grade you got. Are you crazy? Instead I took her arm at the elbow and I said, "Let's get out of here. We'll skip school for the afternoon."

"And go where?" she said.

"Anywhere."

We left by the back door, near the gymnasium, walking down Klammer Road as if we had a right to be there. That was the secret to looking innocent. On Old Black Canyon Highway we stopped at the Laundromat to get Cokes and candy bars from the vending machine, which was Harmony's idea and a good one. Nobody we knew would be there. We both had washing machines and dryers at home, and we both had parents who reminded us five times a day of our lucky existences versus other people's. We talked about that as we walked.

"It's like they think we wouldn't notice otherwise," Harmony said. "Like we're blind or deaf or just stupid and spoiled."

We crossed the highway and walked out into the desert toward Black Canyon Creek and the mountains, away from houses and streets and people. The wind blew Harmony's short hair against her face, and when she tripped over a patch of prickly pear I caught her around the waist. Close to the creek we sat on an outcropping of rock, and neither of us knew what to say. Then she leaned against me, and I thought, great, but she was taking a picture out of the pocket of her jeans. It was of her brother, before he went to Afghanistan, standing in front of their five-sided house on Wanda Drive.

"He looks like you," I told Harmony. He had her black hair and round face, her brown-black eyes with the straightforward expression. He was tall, with long, muscular legs.

"He has prosthetics," she said, "but he's not whole anymore. That must be how he feels."

"Maybe he feels heroic," I said.

"I don't think so."

"That's because you're not a guy," I told her. "We have daydreams of rescuing children from burning houses, you know, where the mother hugs you afterward and tells you how great you are and you say, 'I'm just glad I was there to help, ma'am.' That's what it's like, being a guy."

"You're kidding."

"I'm not," I said.

"If my brother felt like a hero, he would want to see us."

"Maybe he does want to."

"Then why wouldn't he?"

"Because of other macho things."

"Like what?" Harmony said.

"Like he thinks it was wimpy of him to get hurt."

"But it wasn't. That wouldn't make sense."

"That doesn't mean he isn't thinking it."

We sat in the wind with our arms around our knees.

"My brother had a girlfriend," she said. "I mean, he did when he joined the army and went to basic training and left to get himself blown up in Afghanistan. Then one day he got a letter from her, and it was just like the letters a lot of guys were getting, he said, and not just guys but some of the girls he served with, too. An *It's only fair* letter, he called it, as in, *I met somebody else, and it's only fair that you know.* He didn't see what was fair about it. He thought it was fucking unfair, and that was what he wrote her. Only she didn't write back," Harmony said. "She was probably married by then. It seems like everybody is always falling in love with the wrong person."

"Not everybody," I said.

We drank our Cokes, which had gotten warm by then, and I told her that my half brother, Nate, who was staying with us for a while, had had a dog at one time, named Hardy, and that when Hardy died of old age my father had said to Nate, after some time had passed, "Let's get you another dog," but that the only kind of dog Nate wanted was one that would live forever and unfortunately none of those had ever been born.

"He sounds kind of nuts," Harmony said.

"Or else smart."

"Because he knew that everything was going to die one day?" she said.

"Because he decided that it wasn't worth it."

"That might be the crazy part," Harmony said. She unbent her knees and stretched out her legs. "Does that story have something to do with what we were talking about?"

"Well, I thought it did."

"Maybe I'm unrealistic," she said. "Maybe that's the point you were trying to make."

"Unrealistic how?"

"Like I expected to get a C when I didn't write the paper I was supposed to. Like I think people and countries should be smarter than to get into wars. Like I think I'm better than everybody else, self-righteous or whatever, because I know these things and other people don't." She looked down at the rocky wash, and her dark hair fell forward and she was close to tears.

"Maybe there's nothing wrong with you at all," I said.

"Right. Like I'm perfect."

"No. Like, I like how you are."

"Why?" she said.

"I just do."

"There has to be a reason."

"I don't care what the reason is," I said.

I said it too confidently, or else she just didn't believe me. You never say what you really mean to say, I thought. You try to, but the words never fit. Your real meaning stays locked inside you.

chapter twenty-four

SAM RUSH

L EE AND I sat at Byler's Amish Kitchen, just the two of us in the restaurant, with the waitress behind the counter, some distance away. They were due to close for the night. Lee wore a denim shirt with the sleeves rolled up. He had a fresh scratch on his right hand.

"A boxer," he said. "Scared of everything, apparently. Jumped out of a second-story window at the sound of a truck backfiring, the owner told me, and now he's thinking he doesn't want her anymore."

"So you're taking her?"

"I might. Pete's thirteen, and we lost the other two dogs this past year. I don't want the boys losing Pete without having another. Anyway, the dog needs a home."

We drank our coffee and looked out the wide window at Old Black Canyon Highway, which was dark and empty under the streetlights. Occasionally a flash of headlights went past.

"So where are we now?" Lee said.

"There's Nate's neighbor, Mike Early," I said, "whose alibi remains somewhat unconfirmed, that is, his sister and brother-in-law say he was there when he said he was. But they live out of town a ways—nobody living close by, no one to verify his vehicle."

"Maybe this Mike Early left the sister's house after supper," Lee said, "killed Jody Farnell, brought her here, then went back to his sister's."

"Unlikely. His alibi is stronger than that."

"But possible."

"Meanwhile we know that Nate was in the vicinity of Winslow twelve hours or so before Jody was killed."

"You're sure?"

"Positive."

"He said so?"

"Yes, finally. I need to go back up there and check out a few things, and I'll do that as soon as I can."

"Nobody tells the whole truth," Lee said. "Hell, people don't tell me the truth about their animals—what they've fed them, how often they exercise them."

"This is different," I said.

Lee rested his forearms on the table. It was almost unsettling how much he and Nate resembled each other.

"If you think Nate might have done this," he said, "you must think that anybody is capable of anything."

"I don't think he did it," I said. "I just don't know. But depending on the circumstances, yes is the answer. Anybody is capable."

"You think that you and I are psychologically capable of breaking a woman's neck?"

I watched the waitress at the counter. She was waiting for us to leave, and I was hoping she would come over and tell us that, save me from the question. But she wouldn't. She knew me, and she knew Lee. She would let us sit an extra ten or fifteen minutes.

"What I believe is this," I said. "Anybody becomes a murderer the second he performs that action. So a murderer is not a type. A murderer is a human being on a really bad night."

"But you see Nate as being more likely to kill somebody than we would be."

"Is that a real question or an argument?" I said.

"Both, maybe."

"Then yes," I said. "I do. Nate's solitary. He's an underachiever. He's never had a real girlfriend and has had few if any friends. Then there's the fact that he cared a great deal about Jody Farnell, enough to buy her a ring—that was the day before she was killed—and she gave back very little. She gave a lot more to others." When Lee was silent I said, "You asked."

"Nate knew about Jody and other men?"

"He knew enough," I said. "There was nothing about her he didn't take note of. And she was a troubled person. From what I can see, there was a lot to notice."

Lee sat back against the booth.

"It's hard for me not to blame her," he said. "I don't suppose you can see it that way."

"You find out what you can about a victim's life," I said, "and the more you find out, the more alive she seems, and the more alive, the more human. Except that she's dead, and whoever killed her isn't. So it focuses you, wins your sympathy. Plus she didn't kill anybody, no matter what else she did."

"At least not that you know about," Lee said.

"You mean, she might have ruined somebody's life, somehow."

"You don't think so?"

"I don't know," I said. "Sure. Maybe. But that's not against the law. And nobody is predictable. You think you know what you would do in an emotional situation. I think I know what I would do. And we're both wrong."

"I know what I would do sober," Lee said. "I'll add that condition to it."

"What makes you sure you'd stay sober?"

"The number of years since I've had a drink."

"So you'd just leave out the years before that."

"I guess I would."

"That's the thing," I said. "You can't leave out any possibility."

"You don't think there's such a thing as having character?"

"What I think is that everything can suddenly change. We tell stories to ourselves about who we are, and we think that's the final word. What we think about ourselves doesn't necessarily mean shit."

"You believe that."

"Yes," I said. "But so what if I believe it?"

"It's another story, you're saying."

"Yes."

"So nobody and nothing is trustworthy."

"Rain is trustworthy," I said. "Heat and cold. Snow and ice."

"You have zero faith in people. That's what you're saying?"

"*No villain need be. We are betrayed by what is false within.*"

"Philosophy 101?" Lee said.

"Literature 101. George Meredith."

Lee looked outside at the lit-up BYLER'S AMISH KITCHEN sign going off. The night was black without it; the moon was hidden by clouds.

"Sandra called," he said. "She wants to hire a lawyer she knows from the dealership, but Nate has been telling her no. I don't know if Nate doesn't trust the lawyer or if he doesn't want one or if he doesn't want to involve his mother or all three. I don't know what's going on with him. We drive to the clinic and back, most days, and we don't talk. I try, and he doesn't. He looks out the window or turns on the radio. He listens to old stuff, for the most part. He listens to our music."

"I wonder why that is."

"Sandra always played it."

"Sandra called me, too," I told him. "I didn't return the call. I'm already going out on a limb keeping you updated."

"I haven't told her anything," he said, "and I know that Nate hasn't. The one thing he has told me is that he usually doesn't answer her calls. Well, you know Nate and questions. He doesn't like them. To him they're invasions."

"I've noticed," I said.

AFTER WE PAID the check we went out to the parking lot and stood between our vehicles.

"I want to tell you this, so you'll know," I said, "so you'll be prepared. After spending the night in Flagstaff, I believe Nate went back to Winslow in the morning. I have pretty good proof of it. But he hasn't admitted it."

"So he doesn't know you have any proof."

"He does know," I said. "And he's lied to me before."

Lee looked across Old Black Canyon Highway at the desert, which stretched west to the mountains. The mountains were very faintly visible, as if outlined in charcoal.

"I don't know what to do," he said. "I don't know what to do or what to think. The situation doesn't feel real, and I don't like that feeling."

"Nobody would," I said.

"If you were in my place, you'd believe in his innocence?" he said. "Unless or until you knew for an absolute fact otherwise?"

"What else is there to do?" I said.

chapter twenty-five

NATE ASPENALL

J ODY LEFT ON a blustery, gray morning before breakfast. She had told me the night before that she was going, that she would stay with her mother until she found a job and a place to live. It turned out she had already packed most of her things, without my knowing. That was a betrayal, her doing that secretly. It wasn't necessary. I wasn't somebody she needed to tiptoe around.

We were in a restaurant when she told me, a steak restaurant down the highway from the RV park, which she had chosen; it reminded her of a restaurant she used to go to with her father. When she was in the fifth grade her father took her there, ordered her a Shirley Temple, and told her that he and her mother might not stay together. Things didn't always work out in families, he said, and he wanted her to know that, beforehand, just in case. Then he said, "Cheer up, honey. I might be wrong. I might be at your mother's side when I'm an old man."

Tears slid down her face as she told me the story, and I knew they were manipulative, as was her choice of restaurant. Everything had been set up to be about her. But I'm not saying she was aware of that. To the extent that she took care of herself—and I suppose you could call it that—she did it instinctually. She was a genius in that respect. You almost had to admire it. But you couldn't trust what guided her.

We ordered drinks, then two more. Jody was sweet to the waitress, said she was one, too, she knew what hard work it was. The waitress was an older, stout, let's-stick-to-business type who didn't seem to care for Jody, as many women didn't, and it bothered Jody. The more the waitress ignored her, the harder she tried. "Give it up, Jody," I said. "She's busy. She doesn't have time to be nice," and Jody looked at me resentfully, knowing it was more than that. She chose to be irritated with me instead of with the waitress.

We drank and ate too much, which saved us from having to talk.

BACK AT THE RV I didn't sleep most of the night. I tried to hear her breathing without going closer, tried to get a sense of what it would be like, not having her there. I wanted to go behind the partition and beg her to sleep with me. *Please, honey*—putting into motion the maneuver I had almost but not tried with her. What did I have to lose? My self-respect, my dignity, and any chance I might have in the future, which was the only thing that stopped me. I would have sacrificed the rest.

I turned on the television and kept it low. That was what I slept to when I was alone—whatever happened to be on, actors on a screen, music in the background, the idea of life continuing, the idea of it being there to come back to in the morning. Why not start now, I told myself. Embark on your lonely life. I was sorry for myself, which in my view was a substitute for pain—a way to hurt and be hard on yourself at the same time. As I said, I could see my inner workings.

In the morning she was up before daylight, dressing, hurrying, shoving last-minute items into an overnight bag. "Good-bye, Nate," she said. One quick hug and she was out the door. No coffee. No breakfast, her car starting reluctantly in the cold as I stood in the open doorway with the smile I put on my face—no way would I let her see what this was costing me. The white of the exhaust, the dark, brooding trees, the light barely beginning, and Jody driving away from me. I stood there a long time. Perhaps I thought she would come back.

AFTER SHE LEFT there wasn't a moment I didn't miss her—when I heard a moon bird calling at dusk, when I woke to her not making coffee, when I returned to the empty RV in the afternoon. If you've never loved anybody, it won't make sense to you, how disappeared you become. There is absence where there used to be presence, yet at the same time there is too much of you. To say that you feel hollow is to say that you feel full of hollowness. That was my condition. A hole can take up a very big space.

One night at the Chino Valley Recreation Center I talked about Jody to a man named Tom. We were both drunk. He was an exterminator, close to my age, with an ex-wife he was sorry he had cheated on, and when I told him the story about Jody he said, "We could be in Winslow by daylight and take her out for breakfast. I'd like to meet this girl."

We got as far as Cody Boulevard, which is to say, half a mile in the wrong direction, when we realized we were driving without headlights and we couldn't remember how to put them on. "Maybe we should go for breakfast in the here and now," Tom said. We found a Waffle House, had coffee and eggs; I remember thinking, Well, at least I've made a friend. But the next time I saw him he had gotten his wife back, somehow, and he didn't remember that night. Your loss was your own. Hurt wasn't something you could share.

After that I stayed home to drink. It was a cold month, colder than usual; there was snow and sleet, nights when the wind howled, nights when you let the faucets drip so the pipes wouldn't freeze. Sandra kept calling. She said she heard things in my voice. "Let's meet for supper, Nate," she said. "Come on, honey. I don't like eating out alone." I gave in so that she would stop asking. We went to the Mexican restaurant we used to go to, and she told me about a man she cared for and how he cared for her and that she couldn't wait for us to meet. And we would, as soon as he got his life in order and could afford a new truck and could drive down to Arizona from Wyoming. She showed me his movie-star picture. "Can't wait, Sandra," I said, and she smiled, and I pretended to.

When I got home I turned on the electric heater and realized that every second was a hundred lifetimes; you just had to notice. I wanted to call and tell Jody about it even though I could hear her saying, *I don't know what you mean, Nate.* I opened the door and stood with the warmth of the heater behind me and chilly night before me and the silver moon shining above the trees, and I was sorry I didn't have Ernest Sterling to talk to because that was important, to have one person who understood you.

ONCE JODY FOUND a house to rent she emailed me pictures: the wide streets of Winslow, pickups driving down her street at dawn, trains passing on the southern edge of town, their Santa Fe engines picturesque as toys. The house she was renting was blank-windowed and deserted-looking, with a barren yard, yet she had chosen it over me and my RV, which had trees outside and white, winding roads.

Her mother needed her, she said. Her mother needed rides to the pain clinic in Flagstaff, to the drugstore, to the liquor store, to the

Walmart for groceries. Her mother needed Jody to cook for her. Her mother showed her pictures of herself when she was young. "See how I used to be, before your father left me?" Afterward Jody would get into her Toyota and drive to a bar she liked and drink rum and Cokes until she felt like herself again.

"Is the wind chime still in the eucalyptus tree?"

She was calling from the bar. I could hear the jukebox, the whack of pool cues hitting pool balls. She hadn't thought to take the wind chime with her, and I had not thought to give it to her, and at night when I heard the long, echoing melody in the wind, I pictured Jody taking my hand after I bought it for her and the two us walking down the narrow brick sidewalks of Jerome. The next morning I took the wind chime down and packed it up. Jody was already asking, would I meet her in Flagstaff. Would I come see her, and that was why I went the first time, in February. Because she asked me to.

chapter twenty-six

TRAVIS ASPENALL

SUNDAY AFTERNOON MY father and I were driving home from Cave Creek with the boxer pacing in the back of the Jeep when we saw a coyote lying in the desert fifteen feet or so from the pavement. My father braked and pulled over. She had been hit recently, my father guessed, hit hard enough to have been killed on impact and thrown that far.

"People hit an animal and just leave it there," Dad said. "How do you explain that?"

"What are they supposed to do?"

"Call Animal Control, like I'm about to. That's what you do. Or if you live close by, and you're a decent human being, you come back with a shovel. You bury it."

"I guess people don't think about that," I said.

"They don't think, period. That's the point."

In the back of Dad's Jeep the dog was whining.

"Don't be an irresponsible person," my father said to me. "There's no excuse for that. You have to know what it is you're doing, admit to yourself what you're doing, even if it's difficult. That's important."

"I know that," I said.

"Don't just be reactive. You understand what I mean by that?"

"I guess."

"Don't just guess. Either know or ask."

"Okay," I said. "What does it mean?"

"It means don't just do what your emotions dictate. Stop and think. Use your head. Use your intelligence."

On his cell he called Animal Control, then started up the Jeep, which quieted down the dog, although she couldn't seem to stop pacing.

"It's all right," my father said to the dog. "We'll be home soon." But his voice was tense and the dog kept going in circles.

My father had been like that around all of us lately, even my mother, who usually calmed him down, he had told me. That was one of the first things he had noticed about her. "Someday, Travis," he had said, "you'll want to find the person who's going to do for you what you need."

It was late afternoon and sunlight was streaking down from behind the clouds. The mountains looked gray and sort of unreal, like a movie set. We got onto the interstate, and my father watched the traffic while I looked out the side window, from where I could see trails in the wilderness made by dirt bikes and four-wheelers. I imagined myself on the dirt bike I wished I had, flying along with Harmony sitting behind me and her arms around my waist. We could get away from Black Canyon City, from school and our parents, from all the parts of our lives where we were supposed to be a certain way, accomplish certain things, have certain kinds of thoughts. We could take a break from all that, at least for a while, and I started picturing us getting off the dirt bike and making out and my taking off her blouse and seeing her golden skin in the sunlight.

"You have homework for tomorrow?" my father said.

"I've done most of it."

"Well, whatever's left, do it first thing. I don't like you developing the habit of putting things off. If you have work to do, do it."

"You know, Dad, I don't put much off."

"I'm just being a father," he said. "That's my job."

"Well, I'm being fourteen. That's what I'm doing."

Dad was silent. He opened the compartment between the seats and got out a cigarette and buzzed down his window. It was the first time he had ever smoked in front of me.

"This is between us, all right?" he said. "I don't want your mother worrying, thinking this is something I do all the time."

"Okay," I said.

"I don't want you worrying, either."

"I won't."

"Or smoking," Dad said.

"I don't smoke."

"I don't mean just now. I mean, don't take it up in the future."

"All right. I heard you."

He gave me an irritated look, then he stubbed out his cigarette and closed his window.

"It's an easy thing to start, but you get addicted," he said. "Then you're out of control. It's just out of your hands at that point. Drinking is the same problem."

"I don't drink. I don't smoke. But it's screwed up, trying to be perfect all the time."

"You think you're perfect?" Dad said.

"No."

"How imperfect would you like to be?"

"Well, I don't want to blow up buildings or go around killing people or anything."

"What a relief," Dad said.

"So you don't even get what I'm saying?"

"No," Dad said. "I do. That's what worries me."

He got off at the first Black Canyon City exit, as opposed to the one closer to us. He liked to drive down Old Black Canyon Highway through town, take Mud Springs Road under the interstate, then Squaw Valley Road to River Bend and Canyon, where town turned into desert. Community was important, he would tell Damien and me, but it was also good to live outside it.

AT HOME NATE came out of the Airstream and stood with Damien and my mother as Dad let the boxer out and we gave her time to get used to us and Pete and the surroundings. It was almost the beginning of evening by then, and the sky was transparent looking, with a pale, orange tint to it.

"What will we call her?" Damien said, and my father told him that her name had been Belle, like about a third of the female dogs people brought into the clinic. He didn't know what it was about that name that people liked so much.

"Give her a new name," he told Damien. "Give her any name you want."

"I have to think about it," Damien said. "I have to see what kind of name would fit her. What do you think we should name her?" he asked Nate, and my father said, "You come up with one yourself, son," before Nate had time to answer, and Nate said quietly, "That's right, Damien. You name her. She's your dog."

Nate was wearing the jeans he always wore, which had holes in the pockets and knees—not jeans made that way on purpose, like the ones you could buy at the mall in Glendale, but jeans that had ripped from too much wear. Nate was prejudiced against anything new, and he didn't like to spend money. He cut his own hair and bought his clothes at thrift stores. He said that it made him feel sick to walk into a store, especially a mall. Grocery stores were the exception. After all, he said, you had to eat. For a while, though, he wouldn't buy groceries either. He would Dumpster-dive instead. He said you wouldn't believe how much good food got thrown away every day. After he got caught once, he stopped. It wasn't worth getting in trouble for, he said. Stay away from the police, Travis, he told me. It's easy to be misunderstood by them, especially if you're not like other people. Everything they do is based on what is normal versus abnormal. But who knew what normal was? Who wanted to be like most people, anyway? That was how Nate talked, once he got going. Or how he used to talk. He was so different now.

I knelt down and let the boxer come to me, as I had at the clinic. She took a step toward me and jumped back two.

"She's scared still," Damien said. "She doesn't know what we'll do with her."

"We'll be her refuge," my mother said, "like Father Sofie says about faith, during Mass."

"What refuge will Dad have?" Damien said.

"You don't need to worry about me," Dad said.

"What about Nate?" Damien asked.

"Nate comes to Mass with us sometimes," Mom said, "don't you, Nate?"

Nate looked at us. "I don't know that it can be a refuge for me," he said to Damien. "I would like it to be, and I've probably thought about it more than most people have. It's possible that I've thought about it too much. It might be one of those things you need to just fall into, like sleeping or dreaming, and I'm not so good at that. I don't know that I can do it."

"That's a serious answer," my mother said.

"Why put him on the spot like that, Julie?" my father said.

"She wasn't saying anything to me that wasn't true," Nate said.

My father and Nate were facing each other. For the first time I noticed that the expression on Dad's face around Nate was a lot like Nate's expression around Dad: stubborn, almost angry, and at the same time sorry, like there was something they had done to each other that the rest of us didn't know about.

chapter twenty-seven

SAM RUSH

THE OWNER/BARTENDER OF PT's, in Winslow, was a middle-aged, red-haired man with a poorly repaired cleft palate beneath a sparse moustache. He knew Jody Farnell. Said she used to come in three evenings or so a week. One young man or another, and some not so young, would buy her drinks, and she'd play pool when she was asked to. She had a talent for pool, the owner said, but never played for money, not that he had seen. He couldn't recall any man in particular that she spent time with, except for Paul Bowman, occasionally, and Kevin Rainey.

"Tell me about Kevin Rainey," I said, and he said that he was a quiet, sandy-haired fellow, around thirty, of medium height, who did lawn work around town.

"He comes in often enough. Has a few beers, puts money in the jukebox, doesn't make trouble. He's a bit of a loner."

"He lives here in Winslow?"

"I believe he lives in Holbrook."

"How is it you know his name?" I said.

"He did lawn work for my sister-in-law, back when she lived here. That was a few years ago now. She saw him going door to door with his lawn mower, asking for work, and felt sorry for him. You know, somebody trying to scrape together a living."

"She say anything else about him?"

"Well, she started doing her own yard work. I remember that. She said he wanted to be friends, maybe more than friends. Flattering, I would think, since my sister's fifty. But she told him not to come back anymore."

"Did he listen?"

"More or less, I believe."

"What about this man?" I said, showing him a photograph of Nate Aspenall. "Have you ever seen him in here?"

"No," he said. "Doesn't look familiar."

"How friendly was this Kevin Rainey with Jody? Did he pester her?"

"Well, a lot of the men pestered her, if by that you mean stared at her, bought her drinks. He didn't seem much different from the others. Quieter, maybe. He and Jody would talk a little, when he was in here. He would approach her. There was one time he wanted to buy her a drink and she said no. Just no. No reason given. He said, 'Make her one, anyway, would you?' And I did. It sat there all night, right on the bar where I left it."

"How long ago was that?"

"A month or so ago, maybe."

"Did you ever see them talk after that?"

"Once or twice, maybe."

"Did Jody ever say anything to you about him?" I said.

He paused to serve a beer to a bald man in overalls.

"Jody never said much to me about anything. But then my wife works here with me, and I'm careful about how much I talk to female customers, and they're careful about how much they talk to me. I never had a real conversation with Jody. Neither did my wife, for that matter. We knew her. She was here a lot. But we didn't know much about her. I don't believe she had lived here that long."

"How often does Paul Bowman come in?" I asked.

"You don't suspect Paul Bowman of anything, do you? He's not going to hurt anybody. He likes women too much."

"What makes you say that?"

"I've known him a long time, not that I see him as often as I used to. His wife doesn't like him drinking. But when he's here he's talking to whatever female happens to be here, including my wife. He's got a soft heart, my wife says. One night, when he was drinking more than usual—I don't let people get out-and-out drunk, Deputy Sheriff; I keep an eye on that—he told her that he had had an affair with somebody once, and that he would have divorced his wife if the woman had agreed to marry him. But she didn't want a husband, or at least she didn't want him. No name given," the owner said. "No details. Just this sweet spot my wife develops for any man with a heart."

"It's a surprise to women that we have them," I said, and he laughed at that. I had ordered coffee, and he refilled my cup.

"How well do you remember the night Jody was killed?" I said. "It was April 24, a Thursday."

"My wife and I tried to remember, after we heard. We both remembered Jody as having been here early in the evening, maybe seven or eight. Thursdays can get busy, people getting a head start on the weekend, but we were fairly sure she was here, though I couldn't say when she left."

"What about Kevin Rainey? Do you remember if he was in here that night?"

"He was. They might have talked a little. But they didn't come in together. He came in earlier than she did. I remember because he drank more than usual, and I was keeping an eye on that."

"Anything else you recall about that night? Anything unusual?"

"Somebody left their vehicle in the parking lot," he said. "Although that wasn't unusual. It happens all the time. People drink too much, and either they walk home or get a ride."

"Did you know who it belonged to?"

"No. It was a station wagon that I'd seen there before, though."

"An older model, burgundy Buick?"

"Well, it was burgundy. I noticed that much."

"When did it get picked up? Do you recall?"

"Well, it was gone when I came in the next morning to open. That was at eleven."

"Has this Kevin Rainey been in since then?"

"Now that you mention it, no. I don't believe I've seen him."

"You know anybody who knows him? Knows where he lives?"

"Aside from my sister, no," he said. "Not really. As I said, he keeps to himself. You suspect Kevin Rainey? You think he was involved?"

I smiled and said, "I suspect a lot of people. Pretty much everybody."

"Well, I feel terrible about what happened to Jody," he said. "My wife and I both do. We miss her coming in. There was something kind of touching about her. You felt for her, without knowing why."

In the parking lot I checked on whether or not Kevin Rainey had a record. He did, as it turned out, albeit not an impressive one: a DUI and an assault that didn't involve a female. What I couldn't find for him was an address, a registered vehicle, nothing.

I phoned Paul Bowman and asked him to meet me at Burger King, near the interstate, for a sandwich. I wanted to talk to him away from his wife.

He pulled up to the restaurant when I did; we got our food, then sat at a window booth. He wore a tan shirt that was tight across his middle. His fleshy face looked uneasy.

"I know that you frequent PT's bar occasionally," I said, "and that you've run into Jody there at least once. Was that by accident? Or did Jody ask you to come?"

"It was just by accident," Bowman said. "I saw her there two or three times, and we talked for a few minutes. How are you, are things okay with the house, that kind of thing. Nothing special. Nothing personal."

"How about on your side?" I said. "Any chance you went to PT's hoping to see Jody?"

"No chance," he said. "I told you the truth about her. And I don't spend much time there anymore. My wife doesn't like me to. So I'll run out for something at Walmart and stop at PT's for a beer on the way back. If she thinks I'm gone too long, she'll ask me, and I'll tell her. If she doesn't ask, I don't tell."

"Did you ever see Kevin Rainey talking to Jody at PT's?"

"I don't know a Kevin Rainey."

"Well, he's around thirty, medium height, with light hair. Does yard work around town, drives an old burgundy station wagon. The owner of PT's said he comes into the bar now and again and used to talk to Jody."

"Well, there are always young guys in there," Bowman said, "and I'd see them looking at her, but I don't remember anybody fitting that description. I mean, nobody in particular." He took a bite of his Whopper and looked down at his fries. "My wife would kill me if she knew I was eating this."

"So your wife doesn't like you going to the bar because she doesn't want you drinking? Or does it have to do with other women?"

"Both. She can be jealous, like I told you."

"How jealous?" I said.

"We were out of town when Jody was killed. You know that."

"Well, Jody felt threatened by somebody," I said, "and I'm trying to establish who. Maybe your wife took to calling her, warning her to stay away from you."

"Mary liked Jody well enough," he said, "and she knew Jody's mother. You heard her say it yourself. She thought of Jody as a teenager, more or less, and so did I."

"But jealousy is a powerful emotion, and not just for men. In my years on the job I've seen plenty of examples."

"I bet you have," Bowman said. "I've seen Mary jealous. But not over Jody Farnell, I can promise you. Jody Farnell was not the woman Mary was jealous of."

"Who was?"

"A woman from a lifetime ago, and not from here."

"How jealous did Mary get?" I asked.

"Enough to make me miserable, nobody else, Deputy Sheriff. It's me she wanted to suffer."

"On another subject," I said, "did Jody ever mention the town of Leupp to you?"

"Not that I can recall."

"So no idea of her knowing somebody there, or having some kind of connection to it?"

He shook his head. "Leupp is a tiny town on the Reservation, pronounced *Loop*, by the way. I never heard Jody mention it. As I told you, I didn't know much about Jody's personal business. I didn't care to." He drank his coffee and said, "For her sake I wish she'd never moved back to Winslow. For my sake I wish I'd never rented to her."

"I can understand that," I said.

WHEN I LEFT Winslow I took the route Nate Aspenall and Jody had driven the day before she died—north on Route 99, then west on I-5, which was an absolutely straight two-lane road that ran parallel to I-40. The town of Leupp was a shorter drive from Winslow than I had expected, and the town was small, as Paul Bowman had said, cut through the middle by the Colorado River. There was an elementary school, a boarding school, El Paso Natural Gas, Sunrise Airfield, a few businesses, and two churches, one of which was probably the location of the funeral Alice Weneka had mentioned attending. I wondered if it were possible Jody had had a relationship with any of Alice Weneka's relatives in Leupp, back when Jody and Wes Giddens had had their baby, but even if she had, why keep up that relationship, when it seemed that the family had wanted so little to do with her?

I also wondered about the map found in Jody's car and whether it might have been designating a location in or near Leupp, and whether that was why Jody had wanted to drive there. But Alice Weneka knew

Leupp and hadn't recognized it. Unless she hadn't been telling me the truth, but for what reason? I still didn't have any evidence pointing to Wes Giddens, but on the other hand I had not located him yet, nor had the assistant deputy sheriff in Prescott I had asked to help with it.

I drove out of Leupp toward Flagstaff, with a view of the Painted Desert to the north of me and ahead of me the San Francisco Peaks, and from there I took I-17 home. It was after dark when I arrived, and I stopped at the Rock Springs Café, hoping to see Audrey Birdsong, and I did. She brought me coffee.

"It won't keep you up?" she said.

She wore jeans and a blue v-necked sweater, and her hair was in a braid down her back. Her eyes were bluer than I remembered, perhaps because of the sweater.

"If I'm tired enough, I can always sleep," I said.

"I used to be that way when Carl was alive. But now it takes me forever to fall asleep. Too much on my mind, I guess."

"Memories, I imagine," I said.

"No. Not so much anymore."

I ordered the Mexican Combo Plate, and as I waited for it I watched her move around the restaurant. I was the only customer save for two bikers at a booth, and after they left she briefly sat down with me.

"Are you still on Abbott Street?" she asked me, and I nodded. "I miss that neighborhood," she said. "I live in an apartment on Old Black Canyon Highway now, across from the Dollar General. I miss seeing houses when I look out my window, you know, seeing families. But I can't move back. I can't pay the mortgage."

"I thought you sold your house," I said.

"I couldn't afford to. We refinanced, when Carl got sick. We should have known better, but, well, we didn't. I guess I've been lucky to find renters, although renters are a hassle. They come and go, and don't give you notice. And there are always small problems with the house, so it's like you're on call all the time. I see why people hire somebody to look after things. I would, if I had the money."

"I guess it would be different if you had the skills."

"Even then," she said.

I paid the check, and she brought me change and walked outside with me. It was a warm night with a soft wind that caught the brown strands that had come loose from her braid.

"This reminds me of the nights Carl and I went walking," she said. "We used to wonder if we'd see you."

"Did you?" I said, and paused. "Both of you?" I asked.

"Both of us."

"I don't mean to be disrespectful to his memory," I said. "You know that."

"Yes," she said.

We could see the headlights on the interstate from where we stood, and above them the stars that were emerging from the darkness.

"I'm not grieving like I once did," Audrey said. "You have to get over things."

I nodded. Conversing with women was not a skill I possessed. One reason I used to drink, to make an excuse for myself, was that it made me more comfortable around women. Not a lot more comfortable, but some. I had been a drinker when I met and married my wife—so much for comfort, in other words. I had better sense sober.

"I'm in the middle of an investigation," I said, "by which I mean I'm short on time right now, I'm just too busy, but when it's over—"

"I'd like that," she said.

I was getting into my SUV when my cell rang—Leslie Hoover, the assistant deputy sheriff who was looking into a few matters for me, including a verification of Mike Early's alibi.

"I haven't found one, Sam," she said. "But I spoke to Early's brother-in-law and learned something the sister hadn't told us. Mike Early got a call on his cell as they were having breakfast. That was about seven thirty. Said it was a guy who was supposed to work, that day, in place of Mike, saying he could only work until one. So Mike would have to head back. I told this to Bob McLaney, and he got us a warrant for Mike Early's cell, and guess what? The call came from a pay phone in Holbrook. Now why would somebody Mike Early works with in Paradise Valley be in Holbrook?"

I thanked her and thought about it and decided it was too late to question Mike Early by phone. Better to ask him in person, anyway, see his reaction as well as hear it.

chapter twenty-eight

NATE ASPENALL

I DIDN'T WANT TO leave Winslow after I bought Jody the ring. I drove as far as Flagstaff and checked into a motel. I didn't see any sense in driving to Chino Valley only to drive back the next day or the day after that if she said yes. And if she said no, what difference would it make where I was? It wouldn't matter then. Not much would.

My room had a double bed and a picture over the bed of a deer posed in a moonlit canyon. I was on the second floor, facing south, away from the mountains. Beneath the window was a Dumpster and beyond the Dumpster a stand of cottonwoods. If there was a creek beyond the trees, I couldn't see it, although there was still light, a rose-colored stain left from the sunset.

On my way to the motel I had picked up a pizza and a six-pack, and I sat up in bed with the TV on and the sound muted. I felt hopeful, and because of that I drank one beer after another and forgot to eat. Whether or not Jody would call and how soon or how late was in my mind, in spite of her having said she needed time to think. Maybe it wouldn't take her much time. She had lived with me for months, and she knew I had a college education, which would enable me to find a better job, make more money, provide for her as I should. I imagined the house I would buy her someday—a two-story frame house, painted whatever color she wanted, with a nicely equipped kitchen where she would cook for us, or else I would learn to.

I would have been satisfied with us living in the RV, but I wanted to make up for what she had lost in her childhood—a house and family, a sense of security. Maybe I wanted to make up for the family I had lost, too. I used to wonder if the holes and gaps in your life predicted your future.

What I didn't picture was Hannah or any children of our own. That should have been a hint as to how unreal that picture was, that daydream I was having, lying on a bed in a motel room, getting drunk, when fifty miles away Jody might have been . . . but I didn't see that it was unreal. I suppose the alcohol got in the way, and the hopefulness. I had asked her to marry me, expecting her to say no, half expecting her to laugh. Instead she had looked at the coral ring as if it meant something to her that she couldn't tell me about, something she had kept secret from me.

She had gotten her hair cut in a stylish way, parted on the side and straight to her chin, much shorter than it used to be. She was wearing a green blouse and jeans and boots. The men in that small bar were looking at her, watching her as she walked down the hall to the restroom and back. They were envious of me. If I hadn't been there, one would have come over and bought her a drink, sat and talked to her, hoped she'd go home with him. Wherever Jody went, men followed.

There was a good side to that and a bad side, and when I started thinking of the latter I put the room key in my pocket and went out into the night to walk the streets of Flagstaff. It was late, and a light snow started falling, despite the fact that it was late April. I had left the room without a jacket, but I had drunk enough not to feel the cold. I walked down Milton Road all the way to University Drive and walked through the campus. A real campus, not the kind of commuter school that I had attended, where you lived at home, where your life didn't change much from high school.

The campus was hilly, with a creek flowing through it. There were trees and paths and bicycle racks. I sat on a bench across from a dormitory and looked at the lit-up rooms: bunk beds and desks, a girl sitting at a computer, a girl standing at the window, talking into a cell phone. Three long-haired boys walked past me, laughing. Somebody jogged past. I could see a small group of students outside a building, smoking. The late hour didn't matter here. Everybody did what they wanted to. That was what college was for. To leave home and try your wings, to be protected but not, to make that transition in a softer way, so that the shock of the world wouldn't be too much for you.

I thought about the life I had missed, the four years I could have had in a place like that, making my own decisions, forging my own path, becoming who I was meant to become. Why hadn't I? Why had I lacked the courage back then? Why had Lee and Sandra not pushed me? Why hadn't somebody said, This is what you do, Nate? This is how you go about having a life.

But I had missed my chance. You couldn't go backward. As I left the campus and walked back to the motel there was a change in me that I couldn't explain. It was as if I had glimpsed in the sky a spaceship that would save everybody on Earth but would leave me behind. I was a planet in the wrong orbit. I was a whale finding itself in fresh water. I had walked farther than I realized and began to doubt that I would ever get back.

Back in the motel room I did not undress. I lay on the bed and thought about texting Jody just to make a connection, to do it for my sake, not for hers. I pictured what she might be doing at that moment, which was a mistake. It allowed reality in, and now it was there in front of me. She had wanted me out of Winslow, and I knew what that probably meant. There were a hundred ways of lying to yourself, of telling yourself that what was true wasn't, and I had done a great deal of that. The anger began slowly, but once I saw it I wasn't able to stop it.

On television an angry-looking man was standing at an open window in a high-rise apartment building. Below him was New York City, all those lights shining in the streets below. Jump, I wanted to tell him. Nothing in your life is going to get better. Your wife has left you. You have lost your job, your children won't speak to you. Then I looked at his face and realized he looked more lonely than angry, and at that moment a woman came into the room and put her arms around him.

WHEN I WOKE I didn't know where I was. A sound had startled me, and I couldn't identify it—a car door slamming, maybe. Then I was asleep again, and Jody was in bed with me, naked, and I had my hand on the small of her back. I fought not to wake, but your dreams can't keep you in them. There wasn't what you would call real light yet—just the suggestion of it beneath the blue-dark sky with its scattering of stars. I thought about the house and life I had envisioned for Jody and myself, and understood that it was possible to believe and disbelieve, to trust and mistrust, to hope and feel hopeless at the same moment. Somehow your mind could manage those discrepancies. I knew that Jody could be in bed with a man, as I lay in that motel-room bed alone, and I hated her for that. I hated her more than I ever had.

A FEW MINUTES is a long time to have an intense feeling. Hours is what it felt like. You lose track. It's deeper than time. When it subsided the dream began to come back to me, the one Jody trying to replace the other. That's how I would describe it.

chapter twenty-nine

TRAVIS ASPENALL

O N F RIDAY B ILLY Clay wasn't waiting for the bus. At school I learned that Billy's father had been found dead at six that morning. Jason's father was friends with Billy's uncle, who had been the one to find him.

"Vodka and empty pill bottles," Jason said. "Lortab and Percocet. That was probably what he died from, not cancer. They won't know for a while. He didn't leave a note, or if he did, it hasn't been found. His girlfriend was a nurse, and that might be where the pills came from."

"Which girlfriend?"

"The blonde one. The one who looked strung out," Jason said.

We were talking in the cafeteria at lunch. Jason had waited until then to tell me. He said he hadn't wanted to say the words.

"I suppose we have to go there after school," Jason said, "give him some way to get away from his relatives."

"We could hang out in his room," I said, "or go outside, take a walk or something."

We were drinking Cokes and eating potato chips.

"They're going to outlaw this stuff here," Jason said. "Did you hear?"

"I did."

"Un-American, Billy's father would have called it."

I nodded, then I glanced at Harmony sitting with her friends. In English class that morning I had smiled at her, and she had barely smiled back. Now it was Jason she was looking at, and I wondered and thought no. No way. Jason was heavy and had acne. He was uncomfortable around girls.

"I guess we should tell people," Jason said. "I almost told Harmony."

"When was that?"

"Before first period," he said. "She asked me about our math assignment."

"Asked you?"

"I know this is hard to believe, Travis, but I'm not some dumb ass. A few people think I'm intelligent."

"You never know what's up with girls," I said. "You think you do, and it turns out you're completely wrong."

"What does that mean?"

"Nothing," I said. "It's not against the law for one person to talk to another."

We watched two cheerleaders walking past with trays of food, and we watched the geometry teacher checking them out. Then we watched seniors two tables over start a food fight.

"I suppose people will find out," Jason said. "By tomorrow probably everybody will know."

"I guess," I said.

"There's not much to say about it really."

"I know," I said.

In class that afternoon I tried to think of what I could say to Billy. Everything I came up with sounded lame and rehearsed, like from a movie. It all sounded fake, like things I wouldn't want anybody saying to me.

AFTER SCHOOL JASON rode my bus, and we walked to Billy's house on Green Valley Road, a name Billy made fun of; nothing was green in the desert except in and along the washes. There were two cars and four pickups parked at the house, which was small and two storied, with squares of sodded grass in front, newly put in. To the west of the house was a corral for their quarter horse. Billy was sitting on the wooden fence, watching her. When he saw us he got down and the three of us walked in the direction of the Agua Fria with the wind blowing hard against us.

"It sucks, what happened," Jason said.

"It does," I said. "I'm sorry, Billy. I really liked your dad."

Billy nodded, walking with long, slow steps. He was wearing the boots his father had found for him at the Black Canyon City Flea Market last fall. They were Black Jack alligator cowboy boots that cost $1,000 new. "You can give them to your own kid someday," his dad had told him. "Tell him they're from his granddad who was rich as a king at one point in his life."

"I don't think he did what he did on purpose," Billy said. "I believe he would have told me. Not my sister, but honestly I think he would have just come out and said, Here's what I might do someday, Billy, if things look bad."

"Did things look bad?" Jason said.

"No. I don't think so."

We stood near the wash, watching a lizard skim the length of a tree root.

"My fucking mother could have waited to get married," Billy said. "She could have waited until he was well, or else not."

"They've been divorced a long time," Jason said.

"Doesn't matter."

"It was probably an accident, like you say," Jason said. "It's easy to do with pills and drinking. Remember that kid last year?"

"That's what happened then," Billy said.

When we got to the wash we sat and threw rocks at a crushed beer can.

"He was in his recliner when my uncle found him," Billy said. "He was wearing his cowboy hat, for some reason. He had on the hat and gym shorts, like he was kicking back."

"That sounds like him," Jason said.

"It does, doesn't it?"

The sun was hot, and the air was hazy with blowing sand. Over the mountains were high, thin clouds and we watched them sailing east.

"There wasn't a note," Billy said. "So there's that, too."

"Your dad liked to talk," I said. "No way would he not have had his say."

"He could talk to the moon," Jason said.

"He did talk to the moon," Billy said.

We watched a hawk riding the air currents—dipping and curving and rising and falling.

"You wake up one morning, and the whole world changes," Billy said.

"It's unreal," Jason said.

"Except it's not," Billy said.

He stood up, and we started walking back. The wind was behind us. From a distance we saw his sister, Dennie, coming out the back door of the house—looking for us or just going outside.

"She never really believed he was sick," Billy said. "She knew what he had and how long he had had it. He had told us the details. But because she wanted to be stupid about it all, she was stupid."

He walked more quickly, and she stopped and watched him come toward her. When she bent over we saw that she was crying. She was younger than we were by two years, with reddish-blonde hair down to the center of her back. She was athletic, with long arms and legs. I had seen her on their horse, galloping bareback through the desert. She hoped to compete in barrel racing in two years, as their mother had as a teenager. That was only one of her dreams, Billy said. He said she had too many for any one of them to come true.

chapter thirty

SAM RUSH

"M Y HUSBAND'S ASLEEP," Mary Bowman said on the telephone, "and I don't want to wake him, Deputy Sheriff. He's been having heart palpitations. I made him a doctor's appointment for tomorrow. Is there something I could answer for you?"

It was eight thirty in the evening, and in the background I could hear a television playing.

"Here's what I was wondering," I said. "What happens if one of your renters has an emergency when you and your husband are out of town?"

"Well, it just never has happened," she said. "Paul gives renters his cell phone number, and if something does go wrong, he knows a plumber here in Winslow, and somebody who does electrical, but I don't believe he's ever had to call either one. We don't go out of town all that often. We're homebodies, mostly. We always have been."

"You don't have anybody to keep an eye on things?" I asked. "Nobody you trust with keys, just in case?"

"We do things ourselves, that's all. As I told you, we don't have family here. We have just our daughter in Texas. We weren't lucky enough to have more. So we rely on ourselves and do the best we can."

"But after Jody Farnell's body was found," I said, "your county sheriff's department had access to the rental. How was it they were able to get in?"

There was silence for a few moments, then she said, "Paul gave the neighbor a set of keys. I had forgotten about it."

"Paul gave him his own set, or a spare?"

"I believe it was our spare set," she said. "Paul always has his with him."

"Why don't you go ahead and give me your neighbor's name and number, and that way I won't have to bother your husband."

"I suppose I can," she said, "but I don't like to. I hate for you to bother him. He's in his eighties and lost his wife six months ago."

"I promise not to be a bother."

"All right then," she said, "but you tell him what I said. You tell him I was looking out for him."

"While I have you on the phone," I said, "is the name Kevin Rainey familiar to you? He does yard work around town, a light-haired fellow around thirty."

"I don't remember that last name," Mary said, "but there was somebody to come around once, with a lawn mower, wanting work. His looks fit what you're describing. I told him I'd ask my husband, and he wrote down a phone number and the letter *K*. I suppose that was what he went by."

"You're sure it was a *K*?"

"I am. Because it sounded like a girl's name. I mean, if you said it."

"And you gave it to your husband?"

"I did," Mary said. "He threw it away, I believe. 'Don't answer the door for him or anybody else, Mary,' he said. 'You don't know what they're up to.' I'm the kind of person who likes to help a soul out, Deputy Sheriff, but Paul felt strongly about it."

"Any idea why he has such strong views on the subject? I'm just curious. I have people looking for work in my neighborhood, too. Never know what to do."

"Well, it's his not trusting people. It's a safety concern. It makes him angry when I'm ignorant of that."

"You might not want to tell him I was asking, then," I said, and my sense was that she agreed.

AFTER I GOT off the phone I went on my computer and looked up heart palpitations on WebMD, to check what I was fairly sure of already. Stress could cause palpitations, rapid heartbeat, rises in blood pressure, and so on, even in people without heart problems. So what was Paul Bowman stressed about? He had been out of state when Jody was killed, and despite whatever had or had not gone on between the two of them—Jody taking off her blouse came to mind—I didn't get the sense that she was much of a loss to him, except as a renter.

I phoned the Bowmans' neighbor, a man named Sonny Calhoun, and asked him about the keys.

"The Bowmans don't go away often," he told me, "but when they do Paul brings me a set. Not that there's much I could do anymore, at my age, but I'll drive past his rentals once a day to check, make sure things look okay."

"So he's always brought you the keys," I said.

"Oh, no. Only since his house got broken into some months back."

"How long ago was that?"

"At the beginning of February, I believe. He and Mary used to keep the keys on a hook inside a closet door," he said, "and they got taken. Paul had to get all the locks changed."

"Did he file a police report, as far as you know?" I asked.

"Well, Mary wanted him to, but he told me there wasn't much else taken and no real damage done. A few valuables were missing, he said—a watch, I think he mentioned, but nothing to warrant the trouble. He couldn't see the point. He didn't think they would catch the thief, anyway."

"Were there other break-ins in the neighborhood?" I said.

"Not that I know of."

"Where were the Bowmans when it happened?"

"Spending the night in Page, I believe," he said. "Mary has a sister up there."

"You think Paul might have had some idea who did it?" I asked.

"Well, if he did, he didn't tell me."

"Ever heard of a kid named Kevin Rainey? I say kid, but he's about thirty. Light hair, medium build. Does yard work."

"The fellow with the lawn mower, you're talking about?"

"You know him?" I said.

"No. But I've seen him. Never hired him myself. I asked Paul if he knew anything about him, and he, that is, Paul, said, 'Nothing good.' I didn't really need the help anyway. I have a nephew in town."

"So he never did work for Paul."

"No."

"Okay, good," I said. "Now in terms of your checking on Paul's rentals, Jody Farnell lived in the one on the corner of Hicks and Maple.

When the Bowmans were gone to Amarillo this last time, you drove past that house every day?"

"I always check on them just before dark. Everything looked fine to me there."

"Any chance you can remember the night of April 24? It was a Thursday. Did you see anything unusual at that house? Any vehicles parked nearby?"

"Let me think," he said. "The house was dark, as I remember. Don't remember any vehicle in the yard or out front on the street."

"No pickup you recall? A blue Ford F150?"

"Best-selling truck in America," he said. "I own one. I do remember a Ford F150 around the corner, on Maple, though I don't recall the color."

"Anything else you noticed about the truck?"

"There were bumper stickers I couldn't read. I remember that."

"Was anybody in the vehicle?"

"My impression was yes, and I'll tell you why. During my first marriage—my bad one—I used to go sit in my vehicle sometimes to cool off. That's what I figured this fellow was doing. I just remember having that thought and driving on."

"You could see that it was a male?"

"No. I just assumed."

"And you're sure of the date you saw it?"

"As sure as I can be," he said. He was quiet a moment. Then he said, "Now that we're talking about it, I bet that from the rental you couldn't have seen that pickup, but from the pickup, you might have had a view of the rental. Of course I didn't think about it at the time."

Nate Aspenall's pickup, a 2003 blue Ford F150, had two bumper stickers: if you can read this, i've lost my trailer and are you as close to jesus as you are to my bumper? The lettering on both was small. So unless Sonny Calhoun had been wrong about the date, Nate had returned to Winslow after the night he spent in Flagstaff, and he was still in Winslow that evening, a matter of a few hours before Jody was killed. I fought a losing battle with myself not to take some satisfaction in that. I was irritated with Nate's lies, which had come one after the other since the case began. I was spending too much of my time proving what I had known or at least suspected to start with. He had been there. He knew far more than he was telling me.

As for who would have stolen the keys to the Bowmans' rentals, why Paul Bowman wouldn't have wanted to file a police report, and whether this *K* in question was Kevin Rainey, whom Bowman had denied knowing, those were questions I wrote down for later, when I wasn't as tired as I was then. I had been using my days off working the case, as well as my evenings, and I was more than tired; I wanted my life back, such as it had been.

I opened the kitchen door and stepped out to smoke a cigarette before bed. Unlike drinking, I had not been able to quit smoking, although I kept it under half a pack a day.

I could see the back of the house Audrey Birdsong still owned— a one-story bungalow with a detached carport. One summer night, years ago now, I had seen her in her kitchen, in a white top and panties, taking something out of the refrigerator. My wife and I had just divorced, and I had stood there watching her, imagining her life with her husband. If they had been as happy together as I had pictured, which I thought likely, based on my recent conversation with her, that was a good thing. That was something to be glad about, and the fact that it made me jealous was—what? Natural? I could see that. There was the pressure of trying to live up to a memory. Moreover, my track record wasn't a good one. I had yet to make a woman happy for longer than a year.

I went back to thinking about the investigation. It was easier.

chapter thirty-one

NATE ASPENALL

I WAS SITTING OUTSIDE the Airstream when Sam appeared. I didn't
expect him any more than I ever expected him. He suggested we go
inside to talk, and I said fine and cleared off the mess I had made on
the table. I had been trying to fix a model plane Damien and I had put
together last year. Somehow it had gotten broken.

The family had gone to Byler's for supper. When I had said no
thanks, I wasn't hungry, I didn't feel like it, I could see the relief that
Lee and Julie felt. They could go without me; they could get a reprieve
from Nate. As for the boys, who knew what they thought. I couldn't tell
anymore. Circumstances had gotten between us. That was what I was
thinking when Sam drove up.

"Your pickup was seen parked down the street from Jody's house,"
he said once we were seated. "This was late afternoon of the night she
died, Nate. This was the afternoon you told me you were back in Chino
Valley."

I was nervous and he could see that I was.

"You're good at your job, Sam," I said. "Better than I knew."

He shook his head. Dismissing it, I guess.

"So you went back to Winslow," he said. "Why was that?"

My mouth was dry, and I got myself a Coke from the refrigerator. I didn't ask if he wanted one. Then I tried to speak slowly, wanting to tell my part of the story my own way, that is, what happened and in what order, to the degree that I felt mattered.

"In Flagstaff I checked out of the motel in the morning," I said. "I had breakfast at a Shoney's across the street, and as I ate I looked at the Arizona map. Maybe I wouldn't go home right away, I thought. Maybe I would drive north, on the Reservation, maybe to the old Hopi villages. I had never been there. Then maybe I would go to Winslow in the afternoon, I thought, or maybe I wouldn't. Anyway after breakfast I started driving east on I-40 instead of west."

"So you went up on the Reservation first. For how long?"

"From ten or so, I guess it was, until two or maybe three," I said. "I had lunch up there, did my sightseeing, drove around."

"Then what?"

I looked away from Sam. I didn't know how much he knew. Better for me to tell it my way, I thought, than to get sideswiped by a question that I was going to have to answer anyway.

"Then I took State Highway 87 South, in the direction of I-40 and Winslow," I said. "And before I got to I-40 I stopped at the overlook for a view of the Painted Desert."

"The Scenic Overlook Park?" he said. "You saw Jody's car and Mike Early's truck—that's what you're telling me?"

It was clear that he hadn't known, at least not for certain. I went to the door, looking out at the setting sun, feeling tricked, and I had been tricked. I had tricked myself by making the wrong assumption. It was easy to do, and I tried not lose focus by blaming myself.

"You saw what they were doing then," Sam said.

"I didn't see much of anything. I saw Mike sitting in the truck but not Jody. I didn't know what they were doing."

"No conclusions you came to? Nothing you wondered about it, her car next to his, only Mike Early you could see?"

"I wondered, but I didn't know."

I looked down at the model airplane I had put on the side table next to the couch. With one part of my mind I was realizing it was too damaged. I should have seen that. There was no fixing it.

"So you saw their vehicles, and you saw Mike Early," Sam said. "What did you do?"

"I drove to the other end of the parking lot, backed into a space, and waited for them to leave."

"Why?"

"I didn't know what else to do," I said.

"Then you followed them to Winslow?"

I could see on Sam's face what he was thinking and imagining. I can't tell you how disconcerting it is to have people who know you look at you and see a different person. But there was no point in telling him that. He would hear it not from me, but from the person I had become to him. The person I was and always had been was no longer present—not to him.

"I waited before driving to Winslow," I said. "Jody and Mike left at the same time. I figured Mike would leave town, since he had already . . . since they were where they were, rather than at her house, and since they had driven to the overlook separately."

"Then you went looking for her?"

"I went to her house and saw that her car wasn't there," I said. "I waited a while. Then I went in search of her, driving past her mother's trailer, driving through the parking lot of Bojo's and PT's, then going back to her house. I parked down the street and waited, and darkness came and she didn't come home."

"You waited how long?"

"I don't know. An hour and a half, maybe two hours. Then I made the same circuit again, adding the hospital, just in case . . . When I went back to her street the house was dark, and her car wasn't there."

"You must have been angry all this time," Sam said.

"I was a lot of things," I said.

We heard the dogs barking, then Lee's Jeep on the gravel, the slamming of doors, the boys' voices. It was as if I were listening to strangers.

"A lot of things like what?" Sam said. "What else were you feeling?"

"I was worried," I said. "That's the relevant thing. Anything could have been happening to her. I drove back to the overlook, to where I had seen her car last, but it was closed. There was a chain across the road. I went in on foot, and the parking lot was empty. Deserted. I drove back to Winslow and sat in front of her house until eleven."

"Just sat there, all that time? Never saw her? Never saw anybody?"

"I began to think that she was probably with somebody else now, somebody I didn't know, and here I was worrying about her."

Sam was watching me. He was overweight but muscular beneath. He had the kind of build I would have liked to have had.

"So you did what?" he said.

"I drove home in the middle of the night. Didn't stop for gas. Didn't stop anywhere. I would have, Sam, if I had known she was going to be murdered and I would be blamed. But I can't see into the future. I never have been able to."

"Let me tell you something interesting," he said. "Mike Early got a phone call when he was in Snowflake. Seven thirty in the morning on April 25. From a pay phone in Holbrook."

"What did he say about it?"

"Said it was from somebody he worked with in Paradise Valley, who happened to be up in Holbrook."

"Maybe it was," I said.

"I had somebody check with his co-workers, and it wasn't. This is a pretty big coincidence, isn't it? Jody's dead, her car's left in Holbrook, and here he gets this phone call from Holbrook, and the three of you all know each other so well that you saw the two of them together the afternoon before, which was not too many hours before Jody was killed."

"I'm not responsible for coincidences."

Sam looked at me for half a minute or so before he spoke, and I looked directly back at him. I felt like he was daring me to look away, like we were kids in a staring contest. I didn't like eye contact much, unless it was with somebody I trusted, the way I used to trust Sam. That I had trusted him once no longer seemed possible. In fact, I wondered if I were remembering wrong.

"The lying, the keeping information from me, Nate," he said, "makes it impossible for me to think that you're telling me the truth now, or at least the whole truth."

"You think I can't see the doubt on your face?"

"You can't understand that?" he said. "It doesn't seem logical to you?"

"I suppose it seems logical."

"Is there any justification you can give me for the lies?" Sam said. "Anything that would make sense to me?"

I looked out the window at the light in Lee and Julie's kitchen spilling onto the gravel. Whenever I came for a visit, that light was the first thing I would see, and for half a second I was as heartbroken as anybody could be.

"What I think and feel," I said, "my relationship with Jody—none of that is your business or Lee's or anybody else's. I've told you that. It's my right to tell you what I want and no more than that. It's my duty to myself, even. But I didn't kill Jody, and I've told you both that, too, from the beginning. Even if you can't believe that, Sam, Lee should."

"You think it's that simple."

"It is that simple."

"Let's say you're not you," Sam said. "Let's say you're a man who was caught in the act and yet claims to be innocent. You think your father should believe you?"

"That's not the case."

"But what if it were?"

"Nothing follows from a statement not true to fact."

"Where did you hear that?" he said.

"A class in logic."

"So much for what does or doesn't seem logical?" Sam said. "Is that the point you're making?"

"I'm not making any point," I said. "But yes, I suppose so."

"I'm investigating a murder, Nate. That's all. It's my job. The stakes are not high for me, but they are for you. I'd like to see you care about that."

After he left I saw him walk toward the house, hesitate, then get into his SUV. I put my Coke can in the trash, then I picked up the model plane and threw it in there, too.

chapter thirty-two

TRAVIS ASPENALL

"I'M KIND OF interested in Jason," Harmony said. "I'm sorry, Travis. I didn't mean to hurt you."

She told me that at my locker, at the end of the day, then walked down the hall to hers. I looked at my books, the jacket I kept on the hook, my gym clothes, a pair of old gym shoes I had had in there forever, which didn't fit. I stared at everything, trying to figure out what you were supposed to do when the girl you liked didn't care for you anymore.

I told Billy about it on the bus the following morning, on what was his first day back. There had been the funeral, which my parents and I had gone to, then there had been the day his mother had insisted that he and his sister stay home. His sister was still home, and Billy could have stayed out longer, but there was nothing to do at home, he said, except think about it, and he didn't want to think about it.

"Jason's not into Harmony," Billy said, after I told him what Harmony had said to me. "That's what he said to me, anyway."

I was surprised.

"I bet for her it was the army thing," Billy said. "That connection they had."

"I forgot about that."

"When people die, everything changes."

"Harmony's brother's alive."

"Yeah. Well, sort of," Billy said.

He had his hands in his backpack, feeling around for something. He was disorganized, as his father had been. Billy could misplace anything anywhere, and like his father he could get frustrated and lose his temper easily, but also like his father he could find his own anger funny. It was the most likeable thing about him, and different from how I was. It took a lot to make me angry, but once I was I stayed angry for a long time. I had always been that way.

"You need to find another girl right away," Billy said. "Harmony needs to see that you don't give a shit."

"You think that'll bring her back?"

"You don't want her back."

"Then why do it?" I said.

"So you don't care if she sees you looking pitiful, like you do now."

"I don't look that way."

"You do," Billy said.

He had found what he was looking for and held the backpack open to show me—a ziplock bag with a small amount of marijuana in it, maybe enough for three doobies, not that I was an expert.

"You're crazy to bring that to school," I said.

"I found it at my father's and didn't know what else to do with it. Cy looks through my room. He says he doesn't, but that's bullshit. Anyway I'm thinking I'll cut school, leave after first or second period, and go get stoned somewhere, if you want to come. I don't care where we go. It doesn't matter. I don't want to be anywhere. You probably don't either."

"Not much."

"Harmony might just be screwing with you," Billy said. "Making it seem like she's not interested so you'll be more interested. You know how that goes."

"She's not like that."

"Maybe she wants you to think she's not."

"No," I said. "She's not."

Outside the sky was already bright, with the sun coming up earlier. Soon it would be summer. I looked out the window and felt there was nothing to look forward to anymore except life the way it was before Harmony, only worse. I was mad at her, and I had a lot of things in my head that I wanted to say to her. But it felt useless, like trying to break a wall with your hand. It wouldn't get me anywhere. Worse, she would see that it mattered to me.

As we pulled up to the school I wanted to believe that if I went in and spoke to her she would look at me the way she had before. It was possible, I thought, just as it was possible that aliens would land on the school roof, or that when I got home that afternoon Jody Farnell would be sitting at the kitchen table with Sam Rush and Nate. There were a lot of things you couldn't alter. I knew that; everybody knew that. So much for knowing something, I thought.

"Let's not go in," I said to Billy. "There's time enough for us to go out to the parking lot, hang out at the back until everybody's in. Then we can go wherever."

He was nodding his head before I finished saying it.

TWENTY MINUTES LATER we were in the principal's office. We both knew that Billy's father was what kept us from being asked to open our backpacks, what kept us from being spoken to as if it were a crime, our getting caught as we were heading out into the desert. Somebody had seen us, a teacher, probably. Billy was upset about his dad and wanted to talk to me. That was what they assumed, and I guessed that was partly true, although not the way they were picturing it.

"The counselor would like to talk to you, Billy," Ms. Deakin said. "We understand how difficult this is for you, especially your first day back."

"Do I have to?"

"No. Of course not. But it might be—"

"I'll see if I need to," Billy said, "I mean, as the day goes on."

"You just let us know," she said.

WE WERE SENT to class, which was English, for both of us, and when people looked at Billy—everybody knew about his father now—he didn't look at any one person, just sat down and gave me a glance like, Shit, I should have known this was how weird it was going to be.

Harmony was in her seat in the window aisle with the sun on her hair. It was hard to look at her and hard not to. She wore jeans and a red, long-sleeved T-shirt. She had on gym shoes with the laces undone. Mr. Drake was reading to us, and I tried to keep my eyes on our textbook, as Harmony was. "*When you are old and gray and full of sleep / And nodding by the fire, take down this book . . .*" Mr. Drake read slowly, as if he had written it. "*. . . But one man loved the pilgrim soul in you, / And loved the sorrows of your changing face . . .*"

"What does Yeats mean by *pilgrim soul?*" he stopped to ask. "Does anybody have a guess?"

A girl in the first row said, "Does it have something to do with the pilgrims at the first Thanksgiving?"

"Yeats was Irish or something, not American," said the boy behind her, "so yeah, well, no."

"Pilgrims are just people who make pilgrimages," another girl said, "like to holy sites, so maybe this girl in the poem used to do that."

"But why *pilgrim soul?*" Mr. Drake said. "Why put those words together?"

"Because she has a wandering soul," Harmony said, "a soul that's looking for something."

"Such as what?" Mr. Drake said.

"Maybe something that means more."

"Maybe that's why her face was sorrowful and kept changing," a girl said. "She needed what she was looking for. It wasn't this random thing with her."

"So why do you think that might have been appealing?" Mr. Drake said. "After all, other men, we're told, loved her for her beauty. Only this person, this narrator, loved her for this quality."

"Because she wasn't like anybody else," a boy said.

"Well, a girl with three heads wouldn't be like anybody else, either," Billy said, "but this guy wouldn't have been into her."

"Maybe he loved her because he couldn't have her," said somebody else.

"He wanted her because he couldn't be like her," I said. "He didn't have that quality himself. That's why he noticed it in her."

"So at the end of the poem he wants her to do what?" Mr. Drake said.

"Take down the book he wrote," a girl in the back row said, "and dream of how she used to be."

"Yes," Mr. Drake said. "He wants her to *Murmur, a little sadly, how love fled / And paced upon the mountains overhead, / And hid his face amid a crowd of stars.*"

Everybody was quiet, listening or thinking or just sitting there, waiting for the bell to ring. I was just sitting there, too. I didn't look up.

chapter thirty-three

SAM RUSH

I HAD ASKED LESLIE Hoover to help locate Wes Giddens, and she left me a message saying she had; how about meeting her for lunch in the dining room of the Prescott Inn?

She was there when I arrived. She was a tall, slightly heavy woman, ten years younger than I was, with light, curly hair, a pretty face, and a genuine smile. A few years ago I had considered asking her out, then learned that she had a boyfriend. Since then, she had married him.

"I had no luck for the longest time," she said, after we ordered, "then I went over what you had told me about Wes Giddens wanting to start a new life, and I thought, how exactly would you go about that? What would your first step be? And I thought, you'd start by changing your name."

"And?"

"I see that you're just as patient as always," she said, and went on. "That led me to check into who had gone to court, in the past five years, from Winslow, to legally change his name. A lot of people have, it turns out, and Wes Giddens did, four years ago. He had it changed from Wesley Joseph Giddens to Joe W. Weneka, and the only Joe W. Weneka on record who shares his birth date lives in Albuquerque, at 2210 Santa Fe Road. I've got the phone number for you."

"But didn't attempt to call him, correct?"

"You're welcome," she said.

"Thank you," I told her. "But is the answer yes? You refrained from calling him?"

"Of course it's yes," she said. "I know how to do things, Sam. I know the drill. You have a tendency to underestimate people. Haven't I told you that like fifty times?"

"I'm a quick learner," I said, and we laughed.

"I also checked into colleges and universities," she told me, "as you suggested. He's a pre-nursing student at the University of New Mexico, a senior, with good grades."

"Thanks, Leslie. Really."

Our hamburgers appeared, and we shifted the subject to politics at the Yavapai County Sheriff's Department, about which she always knew more than I did. She was smarter about it as well, knew what to say to whom, when, and why. I didn't like politics and didn't do what was in my best interest, as she often told me. She was right, but I didn't see myself as willing to change.

Toward the end of the meal I asked her how married life was, and she said, "Good. Interesting, actually," and that she and her husband were expecting a child in seven months.

"We're both a little on the old side for this," she said, "but what's too old, really, since we got started so late?"

"The next time you feel old," I told her, "remind yourself that you're ten years younger than I am."

After court that afternoon, on the drive back to Black Canyon City, I wondered if I could have made myself sound any more self-pitying than I had.

IT WAS NINE that night before I was able to reach Wes Giddens, that is, Joe Weneka. After I identified myself there was a moment before he said anything. Then he told me that he knew of Jody's death.

"I read the Winslow newspaper online once a week," he said, "and learned of her death three days after it happened."

He was shocked, he said, and he was sorry, but he hadn't known Jody well to start with, and he had not known she had moved to Chino Valley, nor that she had moved back to Winslow. He had not wanted to stay in touch with her. Back then, back when he had known her, she had been in more trouble than he knew. Drugs and so forth. And she had never tried to find him, not that he was aware of.

"How is it you're aware now about her move to Chino Valley?" I asked him.

"It was in the newspaper article."

"Was it?" I said.

"Maybe not in the first article. But there were follow-ups."

"You remember where you were the night of April 24?"

"In a night class of twenty students at Cater Hall," he said, and he supplied me with the course number, the room number, and the name and phone number of the professor.

In response to my questions about Hannah he said that he had a babysitter for her and was planning to homeschool her. She had developmental difficulties.

"Well, you can imagine," he said. "You've probably spoken to Alice Weneka. Hannah was born with health issues."

"What makes you think I've spoken to Alice Weneka?" I said.

"The fact that you were trying to locate me," he said. "It would make sense that you would have contacted her."

"What kind of developmental problems does Hannah have now?"

"It's hard to know where to start," he said. "Balance. Motor coordination. Language problems. She didn't start talking until she was almost four. That's just some of it."

"Yet you don't have special help for her?"

"The babysitter is a student at the university," he said. "That's her field, child development."

"Can you give me her name and phone number?"

"Well, I could, I suppose, but Hannah doesn't have anything to do with Jody being killed. I mean, Hannah was far in the past, for Jody."

"In a murder investigation you never know what will be important," I said. "When questions arise you need answers to them, and here's what puzzles me. I haven't seen a picture of this child since she was three months old. Alice Weneka said that you've never brought Hannah to see her, nor did she seem troubled by that. That seems odd to me."

"I figured Alice told you—I needed a new start," he said. "As for pictures, well, I guess we just had so many other concerns, with Hannah."

"Still," I said, "it seems unusual."

There was a pause.

"Jody wouldn't have hurt Hannah," he said, "if that's what you're thinking. Not deliberately, anyway, not any more than she had already, during the pregnancy. And I certainly wouldn't have. Nobody would have."

"I don't believe a crime has been committed, Mr. Weneka, where Hannah is concerned. It's Jody's murder I'm investigating. I'm just wondering if there isn't something you—both you and Alice—are holding back from me."

"I could fax you a picture, if that's what you need to see."

"I don't believe a picture would do it, Joe," I said. "How would I know it's Hannah? What I need is a reasonable explanation for why nobody has seen this child in years. And why you don't want to give me her babysitter's phone number."

There was a long silence.

"You might want to talk to Alice," he said.

"I have talked to Alice. I'm fairly sure that's not going to get me anywhere."

"Maybe you should speak to her again," he said.

"After the two of you speak to each other? Is that what you're saying?"

"I mean . . . well . . . maybe. But not because we're trying to tell you the same made-up story. It's not like that."

"Why then?"

"Because we both know the truth."

"So why can't you just tell me? Why so much mystery?"

There was silence again.

"Because I don't want to, and I don't have to. And that's my right."

chapter thirty-four

NATE ASPENALL

I DON'T KNOW WHY I went on the Reservation. Maybe I expected something to happen there, some kind of transformation. Nate among the Navajos, the Hopis, the Apaches, if there were any Apaches. Maybe I thought they would see something in me, something white people couldn't see. Or that in a place like Low Mountain or Square Butte or Blue Gap, whose names I was drawn to, I would see my life more clearly and something would wake up in me. But I was just a tourist. I didn't belong, even though I was attracted to the quiet and the openness and felt like a foreigner in my country, as they probably did. I was looking for any reason to form a connection, to not feel left out, as I had on the university campus in Flagstaff. And when I couldn't make a connection something started coming apart in me.

The only person I talked to was a girl at a jewelry stand in Caliente, a soft-voiced girl with long hair and a turquoise necklace. There was a baby on the ground beside her, and that affected me, seeing what amounted to a Jody and a Hannah. Well, what did I expect to find but my own life in all that empty space, on those two-lane roads, in those long vistas? What was I doing there anyway, and why had I spent the night in Flagstaff? In part I had a hangover, but that wasn't all of it. I was separating—coffee from cream, oil from water. I felt as if I was not in control of what I was doing, even though I was driving, keeping my truck between the lines. It's not an easy feeling to put into words.

I drove through Kykotsmovi and Hotevilla, then back through Second Mesa up to Polacca and Keams Canyon, Jeddito and Steamboat Canyon and Burnside Junction. There wasn't a lot to see: mobile homes and concrete houses, a gas station, a black-and-white horse grazing, a cow or two, a child on a broken swing set. I looked at everything I was driving past and tried to figure out what was going on with me. The separation was between a Nate I thought I knew and a Nate I knew just well enough not to trust. Somehow I was newly aware of that, though it seemed to have always existed. But who these Nates were or weren't didn't seem to be the problem. The problem was the distance between them—that they didn't know each other, that they didn't seem to *be* each other. It was frightening but in a remote way, like watching your house burn down and thinking you were in it, but knowing you couldn't be or else you couldn't be seeing it.

I was driving with my windows open to the hot wind and the blue-sky emptiness. It helped that I had to keep my hands on the wheel and pay attention. I had the road to myself most of the time, but each time I saw a vehicle coming toward me, I thought for a second that they were about to come into my lane. They weren't, and I think I knew that, but what was the difference between what seemed and what was? Sentences like that came into my head, and I felt that I was skirting the edges of the subject. I was watching myself trying to keep together what was coming apart. I turned on the radio, and when a voice came on, talking in a different language, I grew calmer. You're all right, Nate, I told myself, whichever Nate you are. It helped me to find humor in it. But there was truth in it, too, in the sense that nothing catastrophic had happened. In that sense I was the same as I had always been.

Then I started thinking, What is Jody doing? Where is she, and who is she with? The anger I had felt in the motel room came back to me, and I thought about the landlord, Wes Giddens, the man knocking on her window, Mike Early, the truck driver Carla Kirby stole from her, even the long-ago boyfriend who watched her dance on a stage. She might be with two at once, for all I knew, and suddenly I had an erection and felt like a pig. A minute later I recalled her trying on rings at La Posada, when she had not expected me to buy her one. Despite the number of men who desired her, not many had been kind to her. She was not a girl who expected much from the world.

There was a sense of unreality to the fact that I had asked her to marry me. It was as if I had done it through a puppet of Nate on my knee. The fact that she hadn't given me an answer was what was causing me unrest. That was what I decided. Uncertainty leaves you hanging, Lee used to say. You'll be all right if you stick to a plan. I didn't have a plan. But I thought that as soon as I saw Jody again I would settle down. I would feel like myself, or to be more specific, I would feel *inside* myself. For the first time I wanted to be inside myself more than I wanted to be inside her. It was funny, but I didn't laugh.

I turned around and drove back to Second Mesa, then south on Highway 87 toward Winslow. There was a dead cat in the road, and I remembered Sandra saying, Just sleeping, whenever we passed a dead animal on the highway. I used to wonder how they could sleep with all those cars and trucks speeding by, and how, in the case of one coyote we saw, it could still be alive when its head was squashed, and when

I asked Sandra, she said, "Animals are not like us, honey. They have magic qualities," and I said, "Bullshit, Mom," perhaps the only time I didn't call her Sandra. For some reason that memory came back to me. The magic and the real and how we boomeranged from one to the other. If I cross my fingers, my dog won't die. Or everything dies and I can't stop seeing it. That was how people were, at the extremes, anyway. Luckier people managed to stay in the middle.

Halfway to Winslow I saw the Painted Desert Overlook sign and turned in at the arrow. There was a long, wide parking lot, perhaps seventy feet in length, with a steep drop-off to the west. I stood at the edge, next to my truck, looking at the mauves and pinks and golds of the plateaus. It was an unusual sight, in that you couldn't see any of it from the highway. There was both the beauty and the unexpectedness of it, which took me out of myself. Whatever I was going through with Jody, I was small. I was insignificant. Then I turned toward my truck and saw the orange Corolla and the white pickup parked side-by-side perhaps thirty feet north of where I stood. I knew who they belonged to. I knew both vehicles well. Jody's was empty. Mike Early was sitting in his truck with his window open, facing the view. I could see him distantly but clearly.

I didn't have to get closer to have an idea of what they were doing. And if I was right, I was being been made a fool of, for which I hated them as well as myself. But I didn't know for sure. I had had those sexual thoughts not long before, an erection and so on; my mind was overactive. I knew nothing, really. I was just wrought up, I told myself. *Wrought up* was what Sandra used to say. I would come home from school—who knew what had happened. Something small, usually, a remark a kid had made. Apparently I used to get into that state.

I drove to the other end of the long parking area and backed my truck into a space. I was thinking that if Mike Early drove out first, I could talk to Jody, and she could explain that she had been asleep on his lap, or that she hadn't been in his truck at all, but walking out to the plateaus beyond where I could see, or that she had been in the wooden building that housed the restrooms. She could explain that she and Mike had gone to the overlook to talk, the way they used to talk in Chino Valley. Mike had a sister in Snowflake, I knew. He sometimes went to see her. Jody, in Winslow, would simply have been on his way. Any of those possibilities were just as likely as the sexual interpretation I had made.

Had I seen more in Mike Early's truck? Had I seen strands of Jody's hair lifted by the wind? No, I told myself. I couldn't have, not from that far. She and Mike Early were friends; that was all. Jody was too afraid to have feelings for any man. That was the thought that came to me, unasked for. Because I had known, almost from the day I had met her, that she was afraid, so afraid that she liked to get as close as she could to the worst thing that could happen. She didn't know how else to feel brave. I can't say how I knew that about her. Her fear wasn't visible, but it had symptoms I was aware of, even if I couldn't say what they were.

Terrified people found each other. That was my next thought—I can't say how I knew that, either. But I thought it possible that I had always had my fears. Deep fears about Nate Aspenall and his life. Fears about finding a place in the world for this oddball whose definition of himself was being part of nothing. I'm not saying that I generally felt afraid. Often in my life I had not felt much. Living alone, for example, I had cooked my food, worked on the RVs, kept those gravel roads smooth, watched television in the evening, went out some, slept and dreamed, like anybody else. Had supper with Sandra, occasionally, visited Lee, stayed in the Airstream. Drove home to Chino Valley, thinking about all I didn't have. Did that come with a feeling? I suppose it had, but I couldn't recall one.

Nothing was going on in Mike Early's truck. I told myself it couldn't be, not with my sitting there. Like my presence determined the world. The strangest thing, the most peculiar thing, was that I didn't once think about walking over there to see. I mean it never entered my head.

chapter thirty-five

TRAVIS ASPENALL

"I F YOU PLAYED any part in it, Nate," my father said, "and you don't own up to it, nobody is going to be able to help you."

"Just say it," Nate said. "Tell me what you think I am."

The door to the Airstream was open, and I heard their voices when I came outside with the dogs to wait for Billy. It was just after supper. I walked quickly toward Canyon Road, wanting to hear but not wanting to be caught listening. It wasn't like them to argue. Nate was quiet, and my father didn't raise his voice the way he told us he had when he was drinking. He had told Damien and me, "You wouldn't have liked me then."

I was almost to Canyon Road when Billy's mother drove in and pulled up next to me. I saw her reach over and put her arm around Billy before letting him out of the car.

It was Friday, and he was spending the weekend with us. Everything was crazy, he had told me on the bus that morning. His father's house had caught fire and everything was lost. The clothes Billy and his sister had not taken out of there yet were gone, along with the keepsakes they had wanted: the tent and sleeping bags from their camping trips to Utah; their father's record collection; photographs of Billy, his sister, and father, the three of them together. Their father had let the insurance on his house lapse, and he had had $73 in his savings account. Not that Billy or his sister cared about the money. It was their mother who did, on Billy and his sister's behalf. She was disgusted, Billy had said. You could see it in her face. Disgusted but sort of miserable, he said, like maybe, underneath it all, and he hadn't finished the sentence but I knew what he meant.

"I tried to walk over," Billy told me now, "but she made such a big deal over it I said, fine, whatever, I don't care."

"My parents hate that word," I said.

"*Whatever*?"

"Yeah."

"All adults hate it," Billy said.

He had on his alligator boots and was carrying his backpack.

"I couldn't wait to get out of there," he said quietly. "Dennie won't come out of her room, and my mother won't quit trying to make her."

I pictured Dennie sitting on her bed, thinking about her dad, wanting to reverse time to last week or last year, wanting what was true not to be.

"I can see why she'd want to be by herself," I said.

"No kidding," Billy said. "But that's a crime at our house."

"Why is that?"

"Who knows? We might be having a thought they don't know about, or make a move they can't see. It's like a jail over there."

The boxer jumped up on him. She jumped up on everybody, which we were trying to train out of her.

"So this is the new one," he said.

"Recluse," I said. "Damien named her."

"How did he come up with that?"

"No idea," I said, although I did know. Damien and I had heard Mom say it to Dad one night, about Nate. Damien probably didn't even know what it meant.

As we got closer to the Airstream I called loudly to the dogs so that my father and Nate would hear, but my father had gone into the house by then. I thought that Nate would come out. When he didn't I said to Billy, "Nate's still staying in the Airstream. That's why his truck is here. He's helping my dad, still."

"Is he," Billy said, but he was fooling with the dog, not listening. Half the time you thought you had to explain things you didn't. People weren't wondering. Their minds were on their stuff.

I went inside for the football, which Billy, Damien, and I threw to each other until dusk turned to darkness. We couldn't have seen each other toward the end if there wasn't a moon and a slew of stars. None of us felt like going in.

When we did my parents were in the kitchen, where my mother was baking, which she was doing for Billy's sake. She made people eat, my father said, when she wasn't sure what else to do.

"How about pound cake and ice cream?" she said to Billy. "How does that sound?"

Billy said it sounded good. Sure he would like some.

I thought my mother might ask us to see if Nate wanted any, but she didn't.

Damien was to sleep on the foldout couch in the den so that Billy could stay in our room. That was the arrangement we had. Billy and I messed around with the computer until everybody was asleep, then we slipped out and climbed to the top of the ridge, where we smoked the pot Billy had brought with him, his father's pot. The moon by then was small, and the stars were glistening. Billy said that last summer he and his father had gotten stoned together one night behind his father's house, near Black Canyon Creek. Just the one time, Billy said. They looked at the stars, ate a bag of Milano cookies, and discussed how interesting it might be to be dead. "Because nobody knows," his dad said. "Isn't that something? Biggest mystery in the world."

The marijuana Billy and I were smoking was stronger than what I had smoked before. The dogs had come up with us and were watching us, for some reason, the boxer, especially, and it began to seem to both Billy and me that we had somehow crossed the boundary between human beings and dogs. They were reading our thoughts, Billy said, and could finally see how hard it must be for us, having only two legs. No wonder human beings were so screwed up, Billy said. Finally the dogs got that. We were crippled, more or less.

"It's all in the physiology," Billy said. "You see what I mean? It doesn't matter what we think or feel. Nothing else makes any difference."

"What's all in the physiology?" I said. I had been thinking about Harmony and lost track somehow.

"Whatever it is I was just now saying."

"You think having more legs would make us smarter?" I said.

"I think being dogs would make us smarter."

"You think dogs are smart enough not to fall in love with each other?"

"It's worse than that," Billy said. "They fall in love with us."

We rummaged in our pockets for the candy bars we had meant to bring with us, and we decided to save the rest of the pot for next time if we were to have any hope of walking down from the ridge upright. Below us was my house and my parents' vehicles and Nate's pickup and the Airstream, in which a light was on and the curtains were open. It looked as if Nate was walking back and forth, back and forth, and suddenly I felt very sorry for him. I felt sorry that Jody Farnell had not wanted him, and sorry that girls were the way they were, picky and not generous, and careless and insensitive when it came to people's feelings. Then there was the hold they had over you because of the way they looked, and the fact that they made the most of it. But I had to admit that there were less good-looking girls you could like, except that you, as in myself, didn't want them. That was how things were.

My thoughts came and went quickly, and it took me a while to notice that Billy's shoulders were shaking and that with his back to me he was crying. From the other side of the interstate was the long, sad sound of a train whistle, and it all seemed to go together, how Billy felt and how I did and the sounds we were hearing and the wind that was blowing. I wanted to tell him that it was all right; everything in the world fit together. I was about to say that when I thought about how it would sound to him, and I knew that he wouldn't be able see to it the way that I did—not now, after what had happened. He was some other place, some place I couldn't get to; there just wasn't a door.

chapter thirty-six

SAM RUSH

P AUL BOWMAN WAS sitting in his truck in the Burger King parking
lot, waiting for me, and we went inside, ordered coffee, and settled
ourselves in a booth.

"I don't have much time," he said. "What is it you want to ask?"

He didn't look good. Paler than the last time I had seen him. He
wore a green shirt and suspenders.

"Where are you about to be off to?" I said.

"Nowhere but home. I'm not feeling up to par."

He showed me the heart monitor he was wearing—a small elec-
tronic box worn at the waist, attached to electrodes taped to him under
his clothes.

"Heart palpitations," he said. "They're trying to figure out what
the problem is."

"I won't keep you long," I said. "I'm just wondering what you have
against a young man named Kevin Rainey. K, you might know him as."

"The lawn mower fellow?"

"That's the one," I said. "The first time I asked you about him, you
said you didn't know him."

"I don't recall that."

"Well, that's the thing about working in law enforcement, Mr. Bowman. We remember what we ask and we remember the answers."

"It's the heart bypass," he said. "It fools with your memory. Ask anybody—anybody who has had one, this is."

"So Kevin Rainey," I said. "How is it you know him?"

"To say that I know him is an exaggeration," he said. "He wanted to do some work for me at one of my rentals, and I said no. End of story."

"Where Jody lived?"

"No. He doesn't know I own that place. Why would he? It was a place I own on Green Street. He saw me there, one day, putting up a mailbox. Asked if I wanted help. Said he could mow the lawn and so forth, and I said no. Like I told you, Deputy Sheriff, I do my own work."

"Even now, after your bypass?"

"Now is a different matter. But I'll hire somebody from here, not Holbrook," Bowman said. "It's how I like to do things."

"So you knew he lived in Holbrook. How was it he happened to mention where he lived, little as the two of you talked?"

"Said it in passing, I guess, the way that people do."

"What was your impression of him?" I asked. "I mean, just generally."

"He seemed all right. Ordinary, I suppose."

"So you're not hiring him wasn't a matter of trust, or anything of that nature."

"No," Bowman said. He wiped his forehead with his shirt sleeve. "My own stubborn character, was what it was." He tried smiling. "I like to think I'm on top of things."

"Kevin Rainey goes to PT's fairly often," I said. "The owner told me that. Maybe you've seen him there yourself. Now I understand you're having memory problems, but is it possible you've seen him there talking with Jody? They knew each other, according to the owner."

Bowman put a hand to his face.

"I might have seen him there, now that you mention it. I can't say for sure, but it's possible. As for seeing him talking to Jody, no. I don't believe so."

"How about other men talking to her?" I asked.

"Well, that happened often enough. Though I don't recall anybody ever getting out of line with her. Nobody was ugly. I don't know of anybody who would have hurt a woman."

That struck a chord with me, and I wanted to give myself a minute to think why. I excused myself, went to the counter for a coffee refill, then visited the restroom, which was when I remembered Paulette Hebson using the same sentence: *I don't know of anybody who would have hurt a woman.* Did either or both of them know of somebody who would have hurt a man but not a woman? Were they talking about the same person? And if so, how was it they both knew the same person, and why were they trying to protect him?

An investigation is like a jigsaw puzzle: when you look at the pieces separately, you can't see the picture; when you look at the picture, you can't see the pieces. But now it came together. If I hadn't been tired, I might have seen it sooner.

I went back to the booth with my coffee.

"I gather that you and Paulette Hebson go way back," I said. "She's the woman you had an affair with at one time?"

There was an uncomfortable pause.

"Three decades ago."

"And Paulette was married then?" I said. "And married when she had the baby? That's why your name's not on the birth certificate?"

He put his hands on the table and placed one over the other. He was shaken.

"Polly was never married," he said. "It's her mother's maiden name she used. Her mother was the one who raised Kevin."

"But he lives with Polly now?"

"No."

"Where then?" When he hesitated I said, "You've already impeded an investigation, Mr. Bowman. And I'm going to find him soon enough anyway."

Two children behind us started laughing, and he waited until they had quieted.

"In the Holbrook Court Trailer Park," he told me quietly. "Number 17."

"And Kevin knows you're his father?" I said.

"Suspects. Doesn't know. Polly had kept a photograph of me."

"And you thought it was Kevin who broke into your house and stole the keys to your rentals?" I said. "That's why you didn't report the break-in?"

"There were tags on those keys, with the addresses, and I had the locks changed right away, so I figured, why add to his troubles? If you've figured out this much, Deputy Sheriff, you're aware that Kevin has had a few problems. They're small ones, but for Polly's sake I didn't want to add to them."

"And you didn't want your wife to know."

"Would you have?"

"Why didn't you want your son to know where your other rentals were?" I said.

"I didn't want him coming to my house, maybe telling my wife who he was."

Bowman looked down at the table, then up at me.

"I have contributed to his support over the years, Deputy Sheriff, just so you know."

"And you lied to me about knowing Kevin because you knew he knew Jody?"

"Kevin wouldn't have hurt her."

"But how did you know he knew her?"

"He mentioned her to his mother."

"So that's why she didn't tell me she had a son," I said. "The two of you were nervous. Is that it? You two talked about it?"

"We worried how it might sound."

"When was it you had this conversation?" I said.

When he didn't respond, I said, "I can check phone records. You're better off telling me."

He looked down at his hands.

"We met at the Little Antelope Tavern in Holbrook," he said. "Shortly after my wife and I got back from Amarillo. We discussed Kevin, thought it best not to mention him. That's all. You have kids, you protect them. But as I said, neither of us felt he was involved."

He put a hand to his waist, on the heart monitor.

"Then why so nervous?" I said.

"My wife. She's made threats. If I talked to Polly, if I saw her, that kind of thing. She won't believe that we stopped sleeping together all those years ago."

"Did you?"

He looked out at the blue sky over Winslow, then at me. His expression gave him away.

"So you and Polly have been friends all these years," I said. "More than friends. You see her and you tell her things, and maybe you tell her about Jody Farnell and you mention details about this boyfriend Jody has in Chino Valley, whose family lives in Black Canyon City."

"No. I never did. First, I didn't know much, and second, there was no reason for me to tell her. Why would I? We had other things to talk about."

"Clear this up for me," I said. "I'm just curious. You tell your wife that Kevin is your son, that you still see Polly, and your wife leaves you, making you free for Polly. Doesn't that make your life happier?"

"Yes. If she wanted me. But she doesn't. I've asked."

He looked at the door opening and three lively teenagers walking in.

"One final thing," I said. "I can't stop you from making a phone call, but I'm asking you not to. As I've said, you've impeded the investigation, held back crucial information—not just you but Polly as well. Don't talk to her until I do. She would be in serious trouble if she helped Kevin leave the state."

"I understand. I don't want to make things worse for her or for me."

"You all right?" I asked. "You need help out to your truck?"

"The only thing I need help with is telling my wife," he said.

chapter thirty-seven

NATE ASPENALL

IT WAS LONELY where Lee and Julie lived, with the wind and dust, the looming mountains, the long stretches of desert. Every morning I woke in the Airstream before dawn, knowing that I could leave before the saguaros and the outline of the ridge behind the house were visible, and that if Sam wanted to come after me, he could. Yet I couldn't move. I'd hear the far-off sound of the interstate. I'd hear the boys outside, walking the dogs. Sounds of life, sounds of normalcy. It was reassuring, even though I was outside of it. There was also how it would look, if I left. I suppose that was the bigger factor.

Then I looked back at the weeks I had been there, and it was like looking at a graph at what it had cost me, and now it was costing too much. I have trouble making decisions, but once I make one it becomes the only thing I see. I've always been that way. I stayed up late packing what little I had brought with me, leaving behind the shirts and jeans that Julie had bought me, none of which I had asked for and none of which I needed or wanted. Once you had more than you needed you had to make decisions, had to find places for things. I liked my life small, clean, and orderly: here is what I wear, here is the pot I cook in, here is where I live. Better to fill a small space than lose yourself in a larger one. I had read that somewhere and believed it.

After I packed, I scoured the sinks in the kitchen and bathroom, cleaned the toilet, swept and washed the floors, stripped the sheets off the bed, and left them folded on the mattress next to my towels. Just like I'd never been there. Nothing of me left behind. I sat on the couch for a while with the television on; then I turned it off and sat in silence. I turned off the lights and sat in dark silence. I thought about notes I could leave: *We don't know each other anymore*, or *You'll never see me again*, or *Nate Aspenall was a figure of your imagination*. They were overly dramatic; I saw that. What bothered me more was that they were an attempt to connect, and I felt I had to leave that urge behind. Therefore, I tried not to think about the boys. I had been nineteen when Lee married Julie, and had watched the family form itself, which for me had been like watching a second heart or liver begin to grow on the outside of my body; but for the boys, I was a natural presence. They had always known me. Don't think about them, I told myself. They don't belong to you.

I got into bed and tried to sleep. On the nightstand was the address of the Sisters of the Good Shepherds Catholic Church in Holbrook, where Jody was buried. I had looked it up on the Internet. The photograph was of a plain, white building that had probably at one time been something else, and there was a glimpse of a cemetery behind it, sheltered by cottonwoods. Jody under the trees, I thought when I saw it. That was better than I had imagined. I heard coyotes howling, and some time later I fell asleep.

I LEFT WHILE it was still dark, turning off my cell phone and keeping my lights off until I was on Canyon Road, and not breathing normally

until I was on the interstate. It wasn't as if I expected Sam Rush or Lee
to appear behind me, or as if I thought of myself as a criminal. But I
liked the secrecy. I understood what a refuge it could be. Withhold,
and people wanted to know what you thought. Stand back, and people
wanted you to come closer. It had taken me a long time to learn that;
it didn't come naturally. My tendency was to be too much out there,
although not socially. I had always been solitary. I meant that I needed
to keep feelings reigned in, not lose control within myself to what I had
lost in the past.

Once I was farther north, in the high desert, it was colder than I
had expected, with a quarter moon hanging low. Just beneath the darkness you could sense the light, and when the red disk of sun appeared
I could feel the shivering of the pickup as the wind hit it sideways.
In Camp Verde I got off the interstate and had a sausage biscuit at
McDonald's, sitting in the bright restaurant, watching teenagers behind
the counter pour coffee and hand early birds their food. I recalled my
first job, which was at a Taco Bell where nobody sufficiently explained
to me how to use the computer/cash register and I walked out after
an hour and a half. I was intelligent, yet I often had difficulty figuring
out what came easily to others. I never expected things to be obvious;
therefore the obvious eluded me.

I got onto I-40 and drove through Flagstaff, where the traffic was
heavy. People going to work, was what I thought about. I kept my mind
off the university. It was just a matter of practice, I thought, just a kind
of mind control. Then I was east of the city and in the flat desert, with
the sun in front of me, just openness and wind and air. Winslow was
ahead, and I decided I would keep my eyes on the highway as I drove
through it. That I wouldn't look at the town that lay just to the south,

where Jody had grown up and made her good and bad decisions, the town she had moved away from and moved back to, lived with pain and caused pain to others, more than she knew. But who would want to admit that to themselves? I saw that simultaneously she had protected herself and left herself open. It was a weird kind of balancing act she had performed. She made herself unlovable and yet was lovable in spite of herself. I had liked her better for what I didn't know she was.

I felt my breathing ease as I left Winslow behind. I didn't look at it in my rearview mirror.

I told myself it was a town I had never seen before. I had learned that you could change how you felt by changing what you thought, even by changing what you knew. Things were not this or that, this fact or some other fact; things were what you told yourself you believed.

HOLBROOK WAS A small, dusty, loosely held-together town of houses and trailers, vehicles up on blocks, broken toys in broken yards. The Catholic church was on East Florida Street, one of the first streets you came to after getting off the highway. A plaque on the outside of the church read: I BIND MYSELF TO THE LABOR FOR THE CONVERSION OF FALLEN WOMEN AND GIRLS NEEDING REFUGE FROM THE TEMPTATIONS OF THE WORLD, which struck me as ironic, unfair, true, and untrue, this iron plaque of worn letters on the white siding of the church.

The cemetery was behind the church, and I found Jody's name on a small, gray stone. The word that came to me was her name, and I said it out loud, if by chance Jody could feel or hear my being there. I did not believe she could, but it was not impossible, and I was open to what was not impossible. Nobody but the dead knew what the world of the dead was like. Jody now knew more than I did.

It's not so easy being a girl. That was what I was thinking, at Jody's grave. They don't believe they know how to be alone in the world, even when they're doing it well enough. They don't trust themselves. They don't feel like anybody. You can see that about them if you pay attention, and I noticed everything about Jody. I accumulated so much knowledge about her that I could feel my way into her thinking and get deeper inside her than she was inside herself. But I had not been able to put my knowledge into her. That had been my biggest failure.

There was nothing on her gravestone, as there were on some of the others: no flowers, plastic or real. Although a sprig of something yellow was lying on the ground beside her headstone—separated from its bouquet, maybe a remnant of what somebody had left for her, her mother possibly, if she had been able to talk somebody into driving her there. More likely somebody had dropped it on their way to another grave. I had not thought to bring flowers or anything else. I had a blue sweater of Jody's at home in my RV. She had left it by accident, and I had kept it. It smelled like the lotion she used. My skin gets so dry, she used to say. Would you put some on my back for me? We did that one night. She took off her sweatshirt and lay on the rug on her stomach. She wore jeans and a beige bra, and she unhooked the bra and I worked the lotion in. It's like we're at the beach, she said. Can you hear the waves, Nate? Can you hear the seagulls crying?

Although I knew how sorry Jody and I both were, I did not have the sense of peace I had expected to find. I realized how unrealistic I had been, about everything. I had moved too far from normal. I didn't want to see that about myself and didn't know how to get away from seeing it. I looked up at the sky, in which white clouds were too great a contrast to the blue. There was no subtleness, no gentleness. The world was a cutting place in which there was no forgiveness. My life had always been some version of that pain, from which I had detached myself. I had a moment of seeing that quite clearly before it disappeared.

I was facing the church and could see the shape of somebody walking past a window, perhaps the window of the church office or restroom. I walked away from Jody's grave in the direction of the older-looking headstones, reading names and dates. 1903–1947. 1852–1900, 1919–1921. The short lives, the infant graves. Then I walked back to my pickup and drove toward the interstate. But once I was on the interstate I couldn't stand the thought of driving back through Winslow, and I got off at the next exit and drove north, on the Reservation.

chapter *thirty-eight*

TRAVIS ASPENALL

E VERYBODY BUT ME was asleep when Nate left. I heard his pickup, and when I went into the kitchen I saw the lights of his truck on Canyon Road just before they disappeared around the curve where Canyon turned into River Bend. I thought maybe Nate couldn't sleep and was going to Byler's Amish Kitchen, which opened at five. But it was a long time until five, and I went out to the Airstream and saw that he had left for real. The Airstream was clean, the way he always left it, and he hadn't left a note, not any place that I could see.

I didn't wake my parents. It wasn't as if Nate was under arrest at our house, and I went back to bed and lay there feeling my heart beating as Billy slept restlessly in Damien's bed and I waited for morning to come.

At sunrise I heard my parents get up. I knew that soon they would notice Nate's truck being gone, and they would go out to the Airstream, and then they would know. I stayed in bed as long as I could. I didn't want to hear them talking about it or calling Sam Rush. I knew that they wouldn't do either of those things in front of Billy, who was still asleep. But Damien was already up. I could hear him moving around in the den, then taking the dogs out.

When Billy woke he and I went into the kitchen. Damien was already there.

"You boys go ahead and have a bowl of cereal," my father said. "Then Mom's going to drive you down to New River so you can hike up to the Indian Ruins. She's got a backpack ready for you. You'll be all right with that, won't you, Billy?"

"Sure," Billy said. "I'd like that."

"Maybe Nate wants to go," Damien said.

"Nate got up early," Dad said. "He's running some errands for me. So the three of you will go. Mom will drop you off and come back for you later."

I would have known my father was lying even if I hadn't known. He was terrible at it. He and Mom both were. During breakfast I noticed him sitting with his head bent as if listening for the sound of Nate's pickup outside. I wasn't listening for it. Nate had a hard time making decisions, but once he made one, he never changed his mind, not that I had ever seen. It was like once he decided something he had to go through with it.

MOM WAS QUIET in the car, and on River Bend I saw Sam's SUV coming toward us in the other lane. He raised a hand to Mom, and she raised a hand back; it looked more like a signal than a wave.

"Maybe he's coming to our house," Damien said.

"Maybe so," my mother said.

On the interstate she told Billy and me to keep an eye on Damien. "You know what the dangers are," she said. "That's free grazing out there, and occasionally there will be a bull. You stay clear of it. Don't fool around, all right? Promise me. And it's a long walk through the desert. Stop and take a drink now and then. I put Gatorade in the pack. And when the day warms up, watch out for rattlers."

"We know," I said.

"I know you know. I'm reminding you," she said. "And don't bring any pottery shards back, no matter how small they are."

"It's illegal and you'll turn us in," I said. "We know that, too."

"I realize you're a teenager," Mom said to me, "but don't be one now, Travis. Give me a break today."

"What's today?" Damien said.

"Irritable adult day," Mom said. "We get to have one."

IN NEW RIVER she let us off at the northern end of Twenty-Seventh Avenue and said she'd be back for us at two—sooner, she said, if we called. We might have cell phone coverage once we were up on the ridge.

The three of us set out, hiking for twenty minutes or so before we reached the wash where people went to target shoot—you could see the wooden targets they left up and the shell casings on the ground—and then we hiked up out of the wash and across the flat desert where a few cows were grazing far to the east of where we were. After that was the gradual rise to the foot of the steep path, with Billy reminding me to stop every so often so that we could have a drink and give one to Damien, who kept falling behind us.

"He's just looking around," I said, "being a kid. He's not really that slow."

"Maybe," Billy said. "But you're walking faster than you think you are."

The three of us made the hard climb to where the ruins were. We had been to the ruins maybe twenty times, but you never got used to what you came upon: the foot-and-a-half-tall circular enclosures, built of rocks, built longer ago than anybody knew, which was all that was left of the walls; the bits of broken pottery you could still find if you went to the enclosures farthest east from the path up to the ridge; the patchwork of houses and desert yards you could see far below; and, most of all, the New River Mountains on the back side of the ridge, which you couldn't see until you were up there. Then suddenly there they were, with their peaks and folds, the crevices the sun couldn't reach except maybe an hour a day, the steep rock faces that nobody, probably, had ever tried to climb.

"What do you think it would be like to hike down into them," Billy said, "you know, to just walk away from everything you knew?"

"Horrible," Damien said.

We sat on the rocky ground in the warm wind, which was strong, up that high. Supposedly the Indians, whichever tribe it was, back then, didn't live up that high all the time. They went only when they were expecting to be attacked. I had the thought that this was where Nate could have come.

Billy and Damien were going through the backpack for what my mother had fixed for us: hard-boiled eggs, apples, trail mix, peanut-butter-and-jelly sandwiches, and another bottle of Gatorade. I wasn't hungry, but I ate anyway. I was hoping Nate had gone to Mexico or Canada, though why he hadn't done that earlier I didn't know. It now seemed a fact to me that he had killed Jody. A second later I was sure he hadn't. My mind was busy. If he did do it, I didn't want him to get caught. I thought it was natural to want criminals to get away. It was an animal thing—don't let the antelope get caught by the lion. Laws were man-made anyway; a lot of them didn't make sense. They didn't give people enough freedom. Then I thought about Jody Farnell lying dead and alone in the wash.

I wasn't aware of how long I was quiet, or that Billy and Damien had started talking—about space, it turned out, and their wanting to visit the moon someday, in whatever spacecraft there would be, by that time, for ordinary people who wanted to see what it was like on that satellite of Earth they had been seeing all their lives in the sky at night.

"Not that we're ordinary people," Billy said. "Ordinary people would rather go to Walmart."

Damien and I laughed, and Billy didn't. He had been making the same kinds of comments he always did, but not as if he thought they were funny. It would be a while before he could. Overhead a formation of Canadian geese flew north. One of their resting areas was Lake Pleasant, which was on the other side of the interstate, not too many miles southwest of where we were. Before Billy's father had gotten sick, he used to take Billy, Jason, Billy's sister, and me camping there and out sailing on the boat he once had. "Leave everything behind," he would tell us. "Don't bring any shit with you when you're out on the water," meaning worries and emotions. He especially didn't like emotions, which was his main complaint about women, since, as he put it, "They're always trying to drown us in them."

Billy's father didn't include Billy's sister in that category. Somehow she was the exception. And while he never kept girlfriends for long, he did have girlfriends, including the last one, the one Jason had said was a nurse. I could see why women might not have liked him. He was a jerk in certain ways. But he was funny and interesting and different from anybody else you knew, and it seemed impossible that I would never see him again.

When it was time for us to hike back we went more slowly, with Damien between Billy and me on the steep path down. It was Billy's idea; it was in his head too much now that people could die. Halfway back across the desert we saw people hiking toward us, and I was sorry they knew about the ruins. There was something about having a place like that to yourself, as your secret. That was the original point about it anyway, for the Indians. They had to protect themselves, be ready to attack before they were attacked. They had to live by their instincts. That was how people were, even though civilization was always trying to civilize that out of you. We had read *Huckleberry Finn* last year and that was on my mind, how things really were as opposed to the way the world was trying to make you see them.

Ahead of us on Twenty-Seventh Avenue I could see my mother's SUV. I could see her standing next to it with her arms folded, and suddenly I wanted to turn and run. I almost couldn't stop myself. But there she was, waiting, and Billy and Damien were behind me, and I wasn't Huck Finn. I was sorry I wasn't, but sorry didn't turn me into him.

chapter thirty-nine

SAM RUSH

WHEN I DROVE up to Alice Weneka's house on North Prairie, she was sitting on her porch swing in a dress and white sweater. She motioned me to a wicker chair, asked if I would like coffee, and came out a few minutes later with two cups on a tray. I asked how her grandson was, and she said he was fine now.

"Children get sick quickly but recover quickly," she said, "lucky children, that is," then waited for me to tell her that I had spoken to Joe Weneka, as he was called now, and that I knew she already knew about our conversation. She didn't say yes or no to that, but waited for me to continue.

"Let's start with what happened to Hannah," I said. "Am I right in assuming that she didn't survive?"

Alice took a drink of her coffee before beginning. She held the cup as she spoke.

"My sister and I are both nurses," she said. "We knew from the beginning that Hannah's chances weren't good. Everybody did. She had an enlarged heart, her lungs had not developed normally, she had fetal alcohol syndrome, mental retardation, most likely, although

that early you can't know for sure. There's a list I could give you. But
her breathing was the immediate concern. We had her at my sister's
house, in Leupp, where we were both looking after her. Wes—Wes,
he was then—stayed there often as well. That's where we were when
she started struggling, and we brought her to the Indian Clinic here in
Winslow. This was when she was five months old."

"So she died at the Indian Clinic."

"On the way."

"Of what exactly?"

"Respiratory failure," Alice said.

"Why didn't you just tell me this the first time I asked about her?
Why all the mystery?"

Alice put down her coffee, went inside, and returned with the death
certificate.

"Because we changed her name," she said. "We gave her my sister's
husband's last name, and for her first name we chose Rowena, which
was Wes's mother's name. *Hannah* had been Jody's choice, not Wes's."

"And you changed her name why?"

Alice looked across the street, where a heavyset neighbor in a red
shirt was soaping his pickup.

"Jody's mother didn't know about Hannah's death, and we didn't
want her to know. We wanted to bury Hannah in the cemetery beside
my sister's church, outside Leupp, rather than in Jody's mother's
church in Holbrook. We wanted Hannah near us. That was important
to us. Maybe Jody's mother wouldn't have raised a fuss, even if she had
known. Maybe she wouldn't raise a fuss about it now, if she knew. But
we didn't want to take that chance."

Alice watched the neighbor rinse off his truck.

"In addition to her troubles with drugs," she said, "Jody's mother had her prejudices. We just thought it was easier this way."

"So the map, then, found in Jody's car? That's showing the way to the cemetery outside Leupp?"

Alice didn't disagree.

"And the symbol indicated the burial plot?"

She nodded.

"Explain the symbol to me," I said, and she went inside again and was gone for a few minutes. She returned with a high school English textbook.

"It's from a poem Wes liked in high school," she said. She showed me the poem.

Western wind, when will thou blow,
The small rain down can rain?
Christ, if my love were in my arms
And I in my bed again!

"What I was trying to draw was *small rain*," Alice said, "but how would you draw that? I didn't know. I'm not an artist. I told Jody what it was supposed to be. I told her that the symbol was on Hannah's gravestone, done by somebody else, better than I could have."

A cool wind was blowing, and Alice buttoned her sweater. She took her time before speaking.

"Jody came to see me after she moved back, and I drew it for her," she said. "She knew the child was dead. She knew the day it happened. Wes went to her house, took her for a drive, and told her. How many of the details got through to her, he didn't know. But she heard it, Wes said. She wasn't going to tell her mother. Her mother couldn't handle it, she told Wes, but we didn't feel as if we could trust anything Jody said.

"Jody looked and seemed different when she came to see me. That was a relief. We talked for a few minutes. She told me she had been in Chino Valley, and she talked about her mother being sick, and that in her opinion drugs were going to kill her mother before long. Then she thanked me for the map, and a month later I read about her death in the newspaper."

Alice put her coffee cup on the tray and set the tray on the floor.

"Do you know whether she visited the cemetery?" I asked.

"I'm hoping she did."

THE HOLBROOK COURT Trailer Park was on Nelson Avenue, not far from the railroad tracks. There were seventeen trailers in all, lined up more or less parallel to each other, with a space of about twenty-five feet between them; no trees, no landscaping of any kind. The windows of two were boarded up; three looked empty. Kevin lived in the green-and-white trailer two from the back. His vehicle was parked in front, but there was no answer to my knock.

The trailer, I had learned, was rented to an Ida Rainey Spencer, in Show Low, now deceased. She was Kevin's grandmother—Paulette Hebson's mother. The owner of the trailer park had told me that Kevin Rainey paid him in cash, each month. "I don't care whose name is on the lease so long as the rent in paid," he told me. The station wagon Kevin drove had been given to him by his grandmother; the outdated plates on it were in her name.

I parked at a distance and waited half an hour or so before Kevin walked up, carrying a paper sack—toilet paper, it turned out to be. He was close in size to Nate Aspenall, but with a more muscular frame. Light hair, green eyes, nice looking at first glance, then a hint of something else on the second. Tarnished somehow. Damaged. Somebody you might not trust if you were a perceptive female. He wore jeans and a white T-shirt.

"Why don't we go inside and talk?" I said.

He turned the door knob—with his left hand, I noticed—and reluctantly let me in. I had expected dismal, but it wasn't in that category. It was serviceable, uncluttered, and clean, although he didn't have much. A brown sofa, a small television. The bedroom door was open, and I could see a made bed and a small dresser. We sat on kitchen stools across from each other at the counter.

"Tell me about your relationship with Jody Farnell," I said.

"The girl who died? I didn't know her very well."

"You'd talk to her at PT's, am I right?"

"I would see her there, sure."

He put one elbow on the counter and rested his chin in his hand.

"As I understand it, you knew where she lived, you'd been over a few times. How did that come about?"

He changed position, then fingered the glass salt and pepper shakers on the counter.

"I was doing yard work down the street," he said. "I saw her move in and asked if she needed help. I didn't realize it was against the law."

"Come on, Kevin. You had a relationship with her. You had feelings for her. I respect that. I'm just asking how things were between you two."

His green eyes wandered from me to his plain, clean living room, which is what he looked at as he spoke.

"We fooled around a little is all that happened. That was twice, maybe, at her house. Then at PT's, well, we were friends. I liked talking to her. She was a nice girl."

"Fooled around as in had sex?"

"We didn't have sex. We did . . . other things."

"Why only twice?" I said. "You didn't want to anymore, or she didn't?"

"She had a boyfriend, by then."

"Who was that?"

"Nate something. He was from before. She had lived with him somewhere. She told me about him at PT's."

"Where was this Nate from?"

"I can't recall."

"What else did she tell you about him?"

"That he knew about me," Kevin said. "How's that? He knew my name."

"She told him about you?"

"That's what she said. She told him my name and where I lived, and I asked her why, and she said she didn't know, that it just came out. And that he was a good person and I would like him. I don't know where that came from. I mean, it wasn't like I wanted to hear about him, and I told her that."

"You were angry then."

"No. Not angry. Sorry."

He followed a crack in his counter with his finger.

"Hard to be sorry and not also angry. Under the circumstances, I mean. Not only does she dump you, she tells you about her boyfriend."

He shrugged. It seemed an unnatural movement for him, a little staged.

"You bought her a drink one night, the bartender said. She didn't want it. Didn't drink it. What was that about, Kevin?"

"She was just trying to tell me it was over between us, that's all."

"She hadn't already told you that?"

"She had. But I thought we could be friends, you know. So what if there was this other guy? I don't get that about girls. If she had liked me enough to . . . well, you'd have to still feel something. I didn't see why we couldn't still talk to each other."

"And she didn't want that."

"No. I guess she didn't."

"Boy," I said. "That's a harsh way to tell you, if you ask me. Humiliating. You buy a girl a drink, and it sits on the bar all night. There must be nicer ways to get that point across."

"It's not how I would have done it," he said.

"How would you have done it?"

"Said yes to the drink but please don't buy me more. Something polite like that."

"So what she did was impolite."

"She could have had that one drink and thanked me for it."

"So here she hurts you, tells you she has another boyfriend, and then she does this. Hurt on top of hurt."

Kevin moved his hand across the counter—his right hand—and scooped up crumbs I couldn't see.

"This was a few weeks or so before she was killed, I understand."

"Something like that."

"Did you see her again after that?"

"At PT's once or twice."

"You didn't want to talk to her about it? Have your say?"

"Not really."

"Why not?"

"What good would it have done?"

"So you considered it," I said.

"Not really."

He got off the stool and opened his refrigerator. I could see a six-pack of Budweiser from where I sat.

"Go ahead and have a beer if you want," I said.

He seemed to think about it. "No," he said, and moved to the sink and drew himself a glass of water before sitting back down.

"The night she was killed, Kevin," I said, "April 24—it was a Thursday. Where were you that night? You understand that I have to ask."

"That was weeks ago," he said.

"Yes."

"I was probably here, alone at home. That's where I usually am."

"Well, the bartender remembers you at PT's," I said. "He says you talked to Jody that night. In fact you left your station wagon in the parking lot."

"Did I?" Kevin said. "Well, I might have. I go there enough."

"How is it you get a ride home when you leave your vehicle there?"

"Usually I don't," he said. "I sleep in the back seat."

"Your mother ever come get you?"

"A few times," Kevin said. "Sure. I'll call her if it's cold enough out."

"What did you and Jody talk about that night?" I said.

He glanced up at me, then down at his glass of water. He took a quick drink.

"I have no idea," he said. "Maybe I drank too much. When I drink too much I don't remember. I turn into an old person."

"Most guys your age get fired up, drinking. That's how I was. Quick to lose my temper and so forth."

"I'm not that way," he said.

I stood up, stretched my back, and took in as much of the trailer as I could. Nothing in view was incriminating or even interesting. Kevin stood as well, his hands stuffed in his pockets.

"Why was it you moved to Holbrook?" I asked. "To be closer to your mother?"

"There's more work here," he said, "here and in Winslow. I worked at a mining operation for a while, until it shut down. For a while I was really making money. I thought that . . ."

"What?"

"That my life was going to get better," he said.

"But it didn't."

"No," he said. "I guess not."

I was looking out the window at the scraggly area in front of the trailer, beyond which was a chain-link fence; a broad, empty street; and a view of Bucket of Blood Drive. It was clearly visible from his window. I debated whether or not to ask if the name of that street had significance for him and decided against it. It was probably no secret in Holbrook that that was where Jody's car had been found.

"Was losing that job when you got yourself in a bit of trouble?" I said. "You have that DUI on your record, and that assault charge. What was that about?"

"That was stupid," he said. "A friend and I got into it. He was drunk and called the police. He was sorry about it later and apologized, told the police it was his screwup. He felt bad about it, and he should have."

"That apology was important to you, it sounds like."

"It's how people are supposed to treat you when they make a mistake."

"Did Jody ever say she was sorry for how she had treated you?"

"No." I had the feeling he said it more sharply than he had meant to. "But she didn't owe me that. I mean, all she did really was move on, like girls do."

After I left his trailer I drove in the direction of Bucket of Blood Drive. Would Kevin have been smart enough to clean Jody's car of prints, inside and out? Well, people watched television. I resented police shows for the unrealistic aspects and the realistic, both—more so for the latter. And unlike a lot of single men his age, Kevin cleaned up after himself, as did Nate, for that matter. And both of them were left-handed, although Kevin seemed to be ambidextrous.

On Bucket of Blood Drive I parked where Jody's car had been found and got out of my SUV. Let Kevin Rainey see me there, I thought. I imagined he would be watching.

chapter forty

NATE ASPENALL

I WAITED AT THE Painted Desert Overlook for half an hour. I sat in my truck with the windows down, listening to the wind as it swept across the plateaus with their muted colors and the blue of the sky reaching down to them. It was after four by then, and the light was changing. To the west there was a quilted pattern of thin, white clouds that trailed off into wisps at either end.

I did not look at Mike Early's SUV or Jody's car directly but held them in my peripheral sight. I believe it's human to not want to know too much. Instead I took myself back to the day before, after we had had drinks at La Posada and Jody drove me to my pickup. I did not leave at once, as she had imagined. I drove down the windswept streets of her neighborhood, past the small houses, the small yards, the fenced-in dogs, the kids playing, the out-of-work men congregated in the short alleys, the quiet streets of Winslow, where Jody said not much happened and not much changed.

People were coming home from work, and a train was going by on the Santa Fe rail line. Beyond the railroad tracks was flat, empty land as far as you could see, all the way to the horizon. I drove past

Walmart and a liquor store, past a pawn shop and a Super 8 and a Burger King. Then I circled back to Jody's part of town and drove past her house, and her car was parked there and nobody else's, and I caught a glimpse of her through the small window, talking on her cell phone. Who was she talking to? Of course I couldn't know. She was talking to her mother, I told myself. She was saying, *I'm just going to stop for groceries, Mom, and I'll be over.*

Only then did I leave Winslow for Flagstaff.

AT THE OVERLOOK the plateaus were becoming inflamed with the approach of evening, and a photo album in my head opened onto Delia Lane and myself on my bicycle, with Sandra running alongside, when my dog Philly ran out into Nightfall Street. Before we could shout her back we heard the squeal of tires. However long ago you lose something the original pain comes back. It did then at the overlook. It was deep and overwhelming—the emotion of a dream that had somehow come into my waking life, then subsided. You could go back and forth between waking and dreaming, I saw, but it wasn't an ordinary occurrence.

A minute or two after that, Mike Early drove out of the parking lot. I saw Jody get into her Toyota, and she sat there a minute, brushing her hair as she looked at herself in the rearview mirror. That was when I started my truck and pulled up next to her, where Mike Early's pickup had been. She was shocked to see me. She looked twice, as if not believing it, and tears came to her eyes. Her expression was a confusion of anger and hurt, and I had not expected that. I had thought she would be defensive, embarrassed, ready to offer an explanation.

I got into the passenger seat of her car. She wore jeans and a close-fitting, gray sweater I had not seen before, made out of a thin material.

Her face hardened into stubbornness. It was as if she had decided: this is what I will do.

"How could you spy on me?" she said.

"Spy on you doing what?" I said.

"What does that mean?"

"It means what were you doing in Mike Early's truck?"

"What are you doing here, at the overlook?" she said.

Her eyes were cold, and I found myself explaining that I had stayed in Flagstaff in order to go on the Reservation and sightsee. That was what I had done, and now I was on my way back. It was the truth, or mostly the truth.

"I bet you stayed in Winslow last night," she said. "Then you parked near my house today and saw Mike Early drive up. He was on his way to visit his sister, by the way. He was just visiting. Then you ended up following us here."

I dug in my pocket and showed her the receipt from the motel in Flagstaff. She wouldn't touch it and I set it in the small compartment between the seats.

"So what?" Jody said. "So big deal. You stayed fifty miles away."

"What were you and Mike doing?" I said. "That's all I'm asking you."

"Talking."

"About what?"

"Nothing special," she said. "This and that, same as always. What difference does it make?"

"Okay," I said. "I was wondering."

"What did you think we were doing?" Jody said.

"I couldn't see you at all. I could only see Mike."

"He's taller than I am."

"I know that."

"What's wrong with you?" Jody said. "What's happening to you?"

"Nothing."

"It's like you're turning into another person."

"I'm fifty different people. Everybody is."

"There's only one of me," Jody said.

"There's you with me," I said. "Then there's you with Mike Early."

I didn't mention that there were undoubtedly others. Already her face was crumpling. But before that, something else flew across it, and I was certain of what she had done.

"I don't want your ring anymore," she said.

She took it off and held it out to me. I could see the indentation it had left on her finger.

"No," I said. "It's yours, even if you're saying forget about all the rest."

"The answer to marrying you is now no," Jody said. "Is that what *all the rest* means? You can't even say the word, Nate. I don't think you would have married me. You don't live in the world at all. You don't know what reality is. There's always been something off about you."

"Like your head is on straight."

"It's straighter than yours."

"How do you figure?"

"I keep trying," Jody said.

"That's what you call it?"

"Now you're being mean," she said. "Mean and ugly and jealous, like most men. I didn't think you would be like that, Nate. I didn't think you would spy on me."

"I wasn't following you, and I wasn't spying on you. I told you that. And here's what I'd like to know, Jody. What difference would it make, anyway, if you and Mike were just talking?"

"Don't put this on me."

"But you were here with him."

"Take the ring back," Jody said.

"I don't want it."

"I would never marry you now," she said.

"As if you would have before."

When I got out of her car, she called after me, "I was going to, Nate. I was going to say yes."

She drove out to Highway 87 in the direction of Winslow, and I watched her go, watched her Toyota until I couldn't see it anymore. Then I drove toward Winslow myself.

chapter forty-one

TRAVIS ASPENALL

M Y FATHER SAID that Nate wouldn't answer his cell phone, not for him or Sandra or Sam Rush.

"Well, that's his choice," Dad said. "It's his right. There's nothing anybody can do about it."

"Maybe Nate didn't go back to Chino Valley."

"No. He did. Sam Rush is aware of it."

We were out on Canyon Road with the dogs. My mother had told Dad after supper, "Go outside. Go do something. You're fidgety." In a lower voice she had said, "You know how Damien picks up on things. Travis is stronger. He knows how to look after himself."

We were crossing the road with the new dog, Recluse, up ahead of us. Pete was keeping pace with us. He was doing all right, old as he was. He didn't want to look bad in comparison.

"What does Sam say about Nate?" I said.

"Not much."

"He tells you a lot, though."

"There's more he doesn't," Dad said.

"How do you know?"

"I know him, and I know how the world works."

He looked behind us, to the east, where the sky was a pale color, like the inside of a shell.

"It seems like Jody hurt Nate," I said, "and probably other people. That makes it not that hard to understand."

"Somebody losing his temper, you mean."

"Yeah."

"There's no justification for violence," Dad said.

"Unless you're fighting in a war, in which case you can get court-martialed for not killing people."

"You've been talking about this in school?"

"In history," I said.

"Well, war is different. Not that I don't see it from your point of view. War is stupid and unnecessary in most cases," Dad said. "But let's leave war out of this."

"I'm just saying I can see how it could happen, losing your temper."

"To that degree?"

"I'm not saying I would do it, Dad, just that I could sort of understand it."

"Understanding it is one thing. Condoning it is another."

"Don't be all Sunday school with me," I said. "You don't even go to church."

"Now you sound like your mother."

We were out in the desert, taking a shortcut to Squaw Valley Road.

"You know how long a prison sentence is for killing somebody?" Dad said. "Even when it's unpremeditated?"

"I thought it depended on some stuff."

"It's a long time, no matter what."

"Well, I know that, Dad. I'm not going to kill anybody."

Dad stopped and looked at the sunset in front of us, the red-orange line along the horizon.

"There's not just the act itself you have to think about, Travis. There's the behavior afterward. Whether the person chooses to say, Yes, I did this. Here's how it happened and why. Not a rationalization, but an explanation, after admitting his guilt."

"Well, you'd be afraid to admit it."

"No excuse."

"But you wouldn't want people to think of you that way."

"Nonetheless," Dad said.

"You mean, you could forgive somebody for doing it but not for not admitting it?"

"I don't like that word, *forgiveness*. I don't believe it has a meaning, outside the trivial," Dad said. "I'm short-tempered with Mom, I say I'm sorry, she forgives me. You don't want to be with somebody who's going to hold a short-tempered moment against you. Anyway, that's forgiveness. But when you're talking about something more serious, it's different. What you're talking about is a matter of disappointment. Losing respect for somebody. Forgiveness at that level doesn't mean much. You can forgive the person, but forgiving them won't necessarily give you those things back."

"Ever?" I said.

"I don't know. Maybe."

Dad whistled to Recluse, who had gone too far ahead, after something, probably. We watched her run in circles, then back to us. She didn't want to get too far away. She didn't have that confidence in us yet.

"Your kids are always your kids, though," Dad said. "Respect, disappointment, that has nothing to do with love."

"Okay," I said.

"You see what I'm saying?"

"Sort of."

We were almost back to Canyon Road, and somebody going past in a pickup waved to us. They had their headlights on, and we couldn't see. Billy's stepfather maybe.

"Then there's the part that would be my fault," Dad said. "That's where the most pain would lie, if you want to talk about pain."

I didn't want to talk about it. We hadn't really been talking about pain.

"What kids get from their parents is undiluted," he said. "I'll give you an example. Let's say that you, the father, the adult, you're lax about a lot of things, you put things off, you don't always pay your bills on time, you're late for work pretty often, but you get by. You get most things done. What happens to your kid is that he can't structure his time at all, can't get his homework done, can't get anything done, not just as a kid but his whole life. He can't organize himself. Kids don't see the subtleties, the degrees. It's all or nothing. That's what they learn."

Dad slapped his hand against his leg, meaning *come here*, to the dogs, and the dogs wandered over.

"I had a temper when I drank," Dad said. "You know that. In the kitchen one night, I picked up a chair and threw it through a window. And there was Nate, watching TV in the living room, seeing me do it. Scared to death."

"What were you mad about?"

"Nothing, Travis. I mean, who knows? Nothing worth throwing a chair through a window over."

"What happened then?"

Dad shook his head. Ahead was our house lit up, and the dogs were trotting toward it.

"I made a big deal out of apologizing," he said. "You know, it was still all about me. Look how sorry I am, Sandra. That's how you get when you're drunk. Center of your own world. Center of *the* world. Don't start drinking, Travis. Smoke pot instead."

I laughed.

"I'm not entirely kidding. But I am kidding. Listen, Travis, you're at a funny age. It's not easy to know how to talk to you. You'll see what I mean someday."

"Talk to me like I'm an adult."

"You aren't one."

"You did before."

"I know that," Dad said. "I probably shouldn't have."

My mother was standing outside, waiting for us.

"That story I just told you, Travis," Dad said quietly, "about the chair, your mom doesn't know."

"You should tell her so she understands Nate better," I said.

"No," Dad said. "Not that one. I don't want her seeing me in that light."

As we got closer Mom looked nervous, and we thought at first that something had happened that she dreaded telling us. But no. Nothing had happened. That was just how we were now, waiting for the next bad thing. Mom was like that now, too.

chapter forty - two

SAM RUSH

I DECIDED TO WAIT a day before I questioned Paulette Hebson. Even if Paul Bowman had kept his word, Kevin would have warned her, and I figured the longer she had to wait for me to show up, the less control she would have when we spoke.

I stayed the night in Flagstaff at a Marriott, a room on the tenth floor with a small balcony from where you could see the dark outline of the hills. I had an early dinner at the hotel restaurant and allowed myself to imagine calling Audrey Birdsong and asking her to make the drive to Flagstaff and spend the night with me in my nice hotel room. There was some small possibility she might have said yes, as in anything was possible. What she would think of me, I didn't know and wouldn't know. It was not in my character to try it.

Up in my room I sat at the desk, itemizing my receipts and figuring up mileage. Then I phoned Bob McLaney at home, which unfortunately he was used to, and caught him up on my conversation with Kevin Rainey and told him my plans for Paulette Hebson tomorrow. Bob was one of the county attorneys who worked with us on our cases from beginning to end, pointed out the legalities, reminded us what we needed in terms of evidence and so on. Bob and I were close in age, and we had known each other a long time.

After that I lay in bed, watching the news, trying to get interested in what was happening in the world, none of it good. I should have called Audrey Birdsong just to say hello, I thought. Why hadn't I? Now the hour wasn't good. Even if she were up, having returned from work, she would be tired. She would have been talking to people all day. But if she had been working, tonight, she wouldn't have been home earlier anyway. With a woman I was interested in, I second-guessed myself. The trust I felt in myself leaked away.

I turned off the TV and tried to sleep.

IN THE MORNING I sat with Paulette Hebson in her small living room. Through the window I could see her automobile graveyard in the morning sun, the light glinting off the metal, the sun shining on the half acre of fiberglass, tires, metal, and glass. She wore men's clothes, as she had before—jeans, a button-down shirt, and work boots. Her shoulder-length hair was roughly tangled. She had been out in the wind, when I had driven up, digging up a patch of prickly pear infringing on the path to her kitchen door.

"I imagine that you've spoken to Kevin, by now, and Paul Bowman," I said. "Let's start with our first conversation and why you told me you didn't have family, you didn't have a child."

"I wasn't much of a mother, Deputy Sheriff. I thought it was time I tried being one."

"By lying about it?"

"By being protective."

"So when you heard about Jody Farnell's death," I said, "your first thought was what?"

"Just that he knew her. That's all. I never thought he had anything to do with it, but he has that record. It follows him."

"So Kevin told you that he met Jody Farnell," I said. "When was that?"

"I couldn't even tell you," she said. She put a hand to her hair and tried to smooth it. "Two months ago, maybe? He didn't say a whole lot. Just mentioned her, really. I asked him how his day had gone, and he said, 'I helped a girl move into her place,' and I said, Who?, and he told me her name."

"When was the next time he spoke of her?"

"Never," Paulette said. "At least I can't recall it."

"In Winslow Kevin goes to PT's fairly often," I said. "Sometimes drinks a bit too much. How many times have you picked him up there?"

"Let's see," she said. "Once last winter, or maybe twice. Usually he'll sleep in the station wagon, but if it's too cold, he'll call me."

The living room was adjacent to the kitchen, and she went in and poured herself a cup of coffee. "Would you like some?" she called out to me, and when I told her no thanks, she came back with hers and waited for my next question.

"So the night of the twenty-fourth and the morning of the twenty-fifth, you were here at home?"

"I imagine I was," she said. "I don't go out a lot. I'm past that age."

"Where was Kevin? Did he happen to tell you?"

"Not that I can remember. But we don't talk every day. Once a week maybe. Sometimes he'll come over for supper."

"So he didn't happen to call you, during that time, or come over?"

"I don't believe so."

"Well, he was seen talking to Jody at PT's the night of the twenty-fourth," I said. "That was the night she was killed."

"Is that right?" Paulette said. "Well, I don't think he was interested in her anymore."

"I believe it was Jody who wasn't interested anymore."

She held her coffee and gazed outside.

"That had to be tough on him," I said. "Don't you imagine? I can tell you from experience that that kind of thing is hard on a man's ego. Then on top of that, Jody was telling him about her boyfriend. Kevin told me that himself."

"I'm sorry to hear that, for Kevin's sake. But girls have broken up with him before, and he's handled it fine, Deputy Sheriff. He gets over things."

"It had to make him angry, though. I understand he's had trouble with his temper in the past."

Paulette put a hand to the back of her neck, under her tangle of hair.

"That friend of his was at fault," she said. "He admitted to that, afterward. Even contacted the police and said he shouldn't have made the trouble he did."

"But there was a fight that took place. The friend ended up with a black eye and a separated shoulder, as I understand."

"That went both ways. Kevin was bruised some as well, but he didn't start it. Kevin doesn't have any worse of a temper than your average person. He never raises his voice to me, and as I've said I have not been much of a mother. He forgives people."

One of her boots had come unlaced and she leaned forward and tied it.

"But you were nervous when you read about Jody Farnell's death. You were nervous enough to call Paul Bowman and ask him to meet you, and the two of you were nervous enough to hide the truth from me."

"It sounds bad when you put it that way." She was trying for light-heartedness, and *trying for* was how it came across.

"If Kevin was involved in Jody Farnell's death," I said, "do you see that it incriminates the two of you?"

"What are you saying, Deputy Sheriff? You have proof that he killed this person?"

"Jody," I said.

"Yes," Paulette said. "I know her name."

She stood and walked close to the window. When she turned back to me she looked sorry.

"I know her name," she said more gently.

"Let me tell you what I know so far," I said. "Jody didn't want to see Kevin anymore. Wouldn't accept a drink from him at PT's, wouldn't talk to him except to tell him about her boyfriend. On the night of her death, Kevin and Jody were seen talking at PT's, and not long after that Jody was killed. That's what we know from the autopsy. Her body was dumped in Black Canyon City, where Kevin knew Jody's boyfriend has family, then her car was brought back here, to Holbrook, where Kevin lives. Not far from his mother's house, and within sight of his trailer. Meanwhile Kevin's vehicle was sitting in the parking lot of the bar in Winslow where he and Jody were last seen."

"But that's not real proof," Paulette said quietly.

I ARRIVED IN Black Canyon City in the afternoon, stopped at the substation, and spent the rest of the day trying to catch up on the rest of my job. Then I had supper at the Rock Springs Café. I knew Audrey Birdsong was working. I had already checked for her car. Another frustration was not how I wanted to end the day.

"How are you, Sam?" she said.

"I've been better, actually," I told her.

She brought me coffee and a menu and said, "The special's good. I can bring you a taste, if you want." She was in jeans and a pink KEEP BLACK CANYON CITY WEIRD T-shirt. They used to sell those at Ron's Market. I was given one by Cy Embrick, and had never worn it. In the opinion of a law officer, anyway, Black Canyon City, like most small towns, was weird enough as it was.

"I'll have the special," I said, "whatever it is. I'll take your word for it."

She laughed. "That doesn't happen to me every day."

"People taking your word for something?"

"A lot of people don't see you when you're a waitress," she said. "I mean, not really see you. My theory is that if you're nobody, they get a chance to be somebody."

"So you're an observer of human nature in here."

"What else is there that's interesting?" She smiled and put her hair up; it was starting to fall out of its clip.

"Tell me about being a pretty woman," I said. I felt my face color. I had not meant it to come out exactly that way. "I'm not saying it as a compliment," I told her, "or not just as a compliment." Embarrassment again. "I just want to know, for the sake of a case I'm working on, why you might stay away from certain men. Not the obviously dangerous ones, but the ones who seem attractive to you, at first, only you sense something and decide to say no to a drink or a date or what have you. What motivates turning them down? What is it you're afraid of happening?"

She slid into the booth and got thoughtful.

"That they won't let you say no to them," she said.

"You mean rape?"

"No. I mean, that if you see them a few times and then don't want to anymore, they'll act as if you're not doing it, like they just won't believe it. Maybe because they feel like they can't survive it or something, and so they can't let it happen. I don't know. I'm trying to imagine what it's like inside their heads."

"How would that translate into action?"

"Following you around, getting angry if they see you with somebody else. Getting violent, maybe."

"Has that happened to you?" I said.

"Not to that extent. But I had boyfriends before I married Carl, and these days, well, you get hit on a lot, as a waitress. So do the others, especially the young ones, and I watch and listen and think about what I see."

"Hit on," I said. "I can imagine. You understand that when I—"

"You're in a different category altogether, Sam."

Then she went to put in my order.

chapter forty-three

NATE ASPENALL

AFTER I LEFT the cemetery I drove on the Reservation, west through Dilkon and Bird Springs to Leupp, then southwest to Flagstaff. It was a long, dusty drive, with the San Francisco Peaks ahead of me looking rough and stark. Instead of getting on the interstate I wound my way through Flagstaff past a hilly park with gym equipment, where I stopped and sat, listening to starlings announce the end of the spring afternoon. Three children were on the playground while a mother watched, and in a grassy field behind the playground I could hear the shouts of boys kicking around a soccer ball. I had my cell phone on the seat beside me, turned off, and I left it off.

The park reminded me of one in Prescott, near where I had grown up. On my twenty-fourth birthday, the day before I moved to Chino Valley, I walked over to the park as a good-bye to the past, a good-bye to childhood, I suppose. A girl I had gone to school with from the third grade on was there, pushing a stroller, and when I said hello she said hello back without recognizing me. That seemed a fitting end to my Prescott life. The next day I moved out.

"I can stay home and help," Sandra said at breakfast, and I said, No, go to work, Sandra. I can handle this. I could picture her face if she were there: the mixture of I-want-what's-best-for-you-honey and I-don't-know-why-you-are-doing-this-to-me-Nate. Perhaps she was unaware of it. It was possible. What I kept bumping into in my life was another person's blindness and how it impaired your ability to hold on to your own perspective. Don't be angry, Nate, I told myself. She can't help it. Look at the pain on her face. In truth there was nothing more maddening, yet somehow there seemed nobody there to be angry at.

I didn't rent a U-Haul; I didn't have much. Chino Valley was not far from Prescott. I could make two trips if I needed to. The RV had a bed and a kitchen table built into it, and I had bought a futon couch, a small recliner, and two lamps at an estate sale I had gone to with Sandra, and she was giving me kitchen things—plates and glasses and cookware, extra things she had. She went to yard sales and estate sales. Everything in our house had belonged to somebody else before it had belonged to us.

It was a hot morning, and I started packing my truck right after Sandra left. I went back and forth between my room and my truck and the kitchen and my truck. I worked hard and fast, and as soon as I was done I drove to Chino Valley and carried it all into the RV, one load after another, until I was sweaty and tired, hungry and thirsty. But I hadn't thought to bring so much as a Coke or a box of cookies with me, and suddenly it began to seem as if the only place in the world there was food was Sandra's house, and only she knew how to cook, and only at her kitchen table was it possible to eat. There I was in a soulless place, with the bare bones of a life. I did not realize then that I was seeing my new life and myself as Sandra might have, or as I thought she might have, which may or may not have been the same thing. There was a picnic table outside the RV and for I don't know how many hours I lay on it on my back, looking up through tree branches at clouds flashing past, or so they seemed; the day was windy and hot.

The first month I remember only pieces of. I ate fast food, did not grocery shop or do laundry or take showers. I must have worked some; that was the arrangement, but I still do not recall it. Eventually, Sandra came by and saw things for herself, called Lee, and Lee came over from Black Canyon City. I'm all right, I said through the screen door and wouldn't open it. Then I suppose I began to do things for myself. As Sandra put it, I "came out of it." It offended me that she would talk about it. I told her I wouldn't meet her for dinner anymore if she continued to. We would meet at the Mexican restaurant where we used to eat so often, even though I didn't want to eat with her there or anywhere else. But I tried not to show it. Be a good son, Nate, I told myself. Don't let her see. "I'll pay tonight, Sandra," I would say, and she would say, "Of course not, honey. But that's sweet of you." It's easy to please women superficially. Beneath that, beyond that, down where they lock their pain away, it's hopeless to try and reach.

THE FLAGSTAFF PARK had emptied. I ended up at a restaurant on Navajo Boulevard called Eddie's, where I ordered barbecue and drank a beer as I waited. I was thinking that I could drive to California or Oregon or Washington and start a new life. Sleep in my pickup until I found a job and an RV or a mobile home or an apartment, and slowly purchase with cash the few things I needed. Even as I thought it, though, it was moving out of sight. I was on my way home.

I was sitting two tables from the window, watching the sky grow dark. There were only a few people in the restaurant, and there were two waitresses. Neither of them was as pretty as Jody had been, or as open-seeming to what life could bring you. The carpeting was a dull brown with alternating squares of green and yellow, the walls needed repainting, and you could smell the disinfectant they used on the tables. I should have kept driving, I thought. I should have waited until I was back in Chino Valley to have eaten, where things were familiar. Home seemed like a refuge compared to where I was now, in that restaurant. Everything changed when you were comparing things, and when you stopped comparing things, well, I didn't know what that would be like. It seemed I was always looking at one thing as against something else— my life before and after leaving home, my life before and after Jody, my life as it was compared to what it could have been. It was possible that I couldn't see anything for what it was.

As I ate supper I watched a mother two tables away trying to get her little girl to eat. "Just one more bite," she was saying, and the little girl in the booster chair shook her head. A little black-haired girl with dark skin and dark eyes—Hispanic maybe, or Navajo. Hard for me to tell. She wore a blue-striped top and had ketchup on her face. When her mother wet her finger and put it to the child's face, the child tried to twist away, but she was caught in that booster chair.

I drank two cups of coffee, then I paid and walked out to my truck. It was full night by then, and the wind was rising, and I was still far from home. I found my way to I-40, then I continued west to Williams. In my head was the vacant-looking rental Jody had lived in and the ring I had bought her. Put that out of your mind, Nate. It never meant anything to her. Then I was on Highway 89, which would take me to Chino Valley.

When you care for somebody you expect it to be returned. I started wondering if love was meant to have that function, or if it got distorted when you tried to make it do what it wasn't meant to do. Maybe love wasn't about getting back from people what you gave them. It might not be about other people at all. It was about opening you up, somehow, so that you could see the world as it was and people as they were. What would Jody have looked like to me if I had been able to see her without expecting anything? The answer was a glass breaking, a moon flying apart, a galaxy trying to hold itself together. I shouldn't have loved Jody, I thought. I should have just loved. Then everything could have been different.

chapter forty-four

TRAVIS ASPENALL

"THE FIRST THING to know about science," Ms. Hanson said, "is that it seems to promise a full explanation for the nature of the universe. How many of you think it does?"

A few people raised their hands.

"So who can give me a definition of gravity?" she said.

"We don't float off into space," Jason said.

"We can't tell that the Earth is moving around the sun at like sixty-seven thousand miles per hour," somebody else said.

"But are those definitions of gravity, or are they descriptions?"

"Descriptions."

"Right," Ms. Hanson said. "Isaac Newton wrote, 'the cause of gravity is what I do not pretend to know.'"

"So what is the definition?"

"That's the point," Ms. Hanson said. "Nobody knows. Everything in the universe at some level becomes a mystery."

"For now, though, or for always?"

"Anybody want to guess the answer to that?" Ms. Hanson said.

"I will," somebody else said. "It's a mystery."

"Why become a scientist then?" Billy said. "Why bother?"

"Because you could figure out just one more thing," Harmony said.

"How are you supposed to live with all that unknowing?" somebody behind me asked.

"You're already living with it," Billy said. "You can't count on anything. You don't know how long you're going to live or how you're going to die. You don't know a fucking lot of things."

"Billy Clay," Ms. Hanson said.

"Well, you don't, do you?"

"No," Ms. Hanson said. "But do you have to use that particular word to say it?"

"Well, in terms of what I was saying, shit, yes," Billy said.

Everybody laughed, including her. She didn't like profanity, but she knew smart when she heard it.

On the bus that afternoon Billy said, "I might be done with honors classes. My grades suck, and I'm tired of working so hard. Who cares, anyway? My mother's new son can be the brains of the family."

"You mean one of Cy's kids?" I said.

"Yes. But not one he has already."

"You're kidding me," I said.

"She's forty-six. I mean, who would think?"

"Was it on purpose?"

"Fuck. I hope not."

He looked out the window at the dusty sky.

"Cy says he's going to build us a bigger house, maybe with a pool," Billy said. "This would be somewhere on the other side of the interstate. Some new street I've never heard of. So there goes taking the bus with my friends."

"Maybe it will never happen."

"No," Billy said. "Not with Cy. That's what would have happened with my dad."

We got off at the same stop and walked the mile or so to what was left of his father's house. Most of the rubbish had been cleared away, and there was only the foundation left and the brick fireplace, which they had never used. Sand had blown across the concrete, and Billy marked off with a stick where the living room used to be, the kitchen, and the bedrooms.

"Here is where my dad was found," he said, and drew a picture of the recliner in the living room. "He died where he wanted to be, doing what he liked to do."

"Drinking, you mean?"

"And drugs," Billy said. "He was into pills before he got sick. I found his stash once, a long time ago. I was so young and stupid I didn't take any."

He drew a picture of the concrete Buddha statue his dad used to have sitting on the hearth.

"That's a smart hiding place," I said.

"I was trying to move it over, I can't remember why. I expected it to be heavy, but it was hollow inside, and there they were, stuffed inside a pea can. Peas," he said, "like you would eat."

"Painkillers, peas, peace," I said.

"Right."

"Did the Buddha burn?" I asked.

"It got blackened. Dennie has it in her closet."

We headed back. The sun was low behind us, but in front of us the day was bright, as if we were walking backward, toward lunch instead of supper, toward last year instead of next year, as if with each step we were undoing the past, even though it meant we would have to do all those same things again. We wouldn't be able to change anything. That was how science worked. You could make discoveries, which could make things better in the future, but you couldn't undo anything that had happened or had been set in motion. It was the one sad fact about the universe.

WHEN I GOT home my mother was in the Airstream, ripping up a corner of the brown carpeting.

"I want to redo in here," she said. "It's dated and worn. Depressing looking. When Billy comes to spend the night, you and he could stay out here. A bit like camping."

She looked down at the carpeting. "I suppose we could have just gotten it cleaned," she said, "but I think we'd be better off starting over. What do you think?"

It wasn't a real question.

"Okay then. You can get started before supper. I'll leave it to you," she said, as I had known she would. That was how she got us to do what she wanted done.

I put the radio on and listened to country-and-western while I worked—music that Harmony didn't like. All those cowboys who hate Indians, she used to say. All those pretend heartachy people. As for the heartachy part, well, nobody had damaged hers yet. She might say something different when and if that happened. Maybe Jason would break up with her at some point, I thought. He was going out with her now. He had not come out and said that, but it was obvious.

When my father got home from work he came into the Airstream to see what I had done and to tell me how I should have done it instead.

"It's fine, though," he said. "It'll work." One sleeve of his shirt was ripped. "Doberman mix," he said. "Don't become a vet, Travis. Animals hate us."

"I wasn't going to."

"What field might you go into then? Do you think about it?"

"Not really."

"You might want to start. Time moves fast."

"I thought I'd be a teenager a while longer."

"I was afraid of that," Dad said.

Just before I went in for supper I moved the bed out of the back corner, and just under the edge of the carpeting was where I found the coral ring. It was a smallish, woman's ring, and I was pretty sure that Nate had bought it for Jody Farnell. Sam Rush had told my father about it, and he had told me. "That's how much Nate cared for her," my father had said.

I put the ring in my pocket and tried to figure out what to do with it.

chapter forty-five

SAM RUSH

WITH MY SLIDING glass door open to the night wind, I sat at my kitchen table in front of my computer, preparing for my meeting in Prescott with Bob McLaney. I had typed up my notes from the beginning of the investigation and emailed them to him, including my recent conversation with Paulette Hebson. Now I wanted to familiarize myself with the information and make sure of the correct sequence of events. I drank coffee in order to keep myself alert, and when I made changes on the computer, typing with two fingers, I wished not for the first time that I had taken a typing class in high school.

By one in the morning I had done what I could, and I went outside. My neighborhood was asleep. It was mostly older folks, aside from a young couple down the street who partied late and had too much company. But tonight even their lights were out. There was a white moon, and I focused on it and tried to let my mind empty, especially of Lee and Julie Aspenall. I was sorry I had taken on the case, yet I understood what my reasoning had been, and it still made sense to me. A sense of certainty belongs to your twenties and thirties. After that, you make do with the complexities of being human. I went inside and lay on the couch and fell asleep in front of the television.

On the drive to Prescott in the morning I had my paperwork on the passenger seat, and I went over the investigation one more time in my mind, trying to see what if anything I had overlooked, not given enough significance to, or not followed up on. In the back of my mind was Jody Farnell in her Toyota, a girl on her own who knew too many men, in too many different ways, stopping at PT's in the early evening. Despite how much we knew, we still knew too little. But unless you had a confession or indisputable physical evidence, there was always the chance that anything could have happened.

THE MORNING WAS warm and cloudless when I left Black Canyon City. Prescott was considerably cooler, with low clouds hanging raggedly over the hills. Bob's office was upstairs from the Sheriff's Department. I could remember when the county attorneys had their offices in the pretty courthouse across the street, as could Bob.

He was waiting for me, wearing jeans and a black Western shirt— not one of his days to be in court. He was a few inches shorter than I was, darker complected and thinner, with brown hair mixed with gray, a focused, sharp expression, and a sense of humor you didn't expect. I had gotten us two coffees, and I handed one to him and sat in the chair opposite his desk.

"You look tired," he said.

"I bet."

"Myself," he said, "we had a crying grandchild staying with us. Seven months old, with strong lungs. Guess whose bed he slept in."

Then we looked at our notes and started talking about the case.

"We have a fair amount of evidence against Nate Aspenall," he said, "even though it's circumstantial. Nate has history with Jody, is fixated on her big-time, sees her at the overlook performing a sexual act with Mike Early one day after he proposes to her, she ends up dead five hours or so later, his pickup is parked near her house—all night, possibly—and somebody makes a phone call the next morning to Mike Early from the town in which Jody's car is found."

Bob took a drink of coffee. "The fact that Jody's body was found near Nate's father's house could go either way, I suppose, although I tend to see it as strong. How about you?"

"Leaving her body close to somebody he has ties to," I said, "that was my thinking. So that he doesn't feel as if he's just abandoning it. Plus he doesn't just throw it in the wash—he can't bring himself to. But he likes the idea of tossing her away, now that he's been tossed aside by her. So he positions her that way. It's the closest he can come.

"Since we're assuming unpremeditated," I said, "it's possible he had a need to be caught. He's horrified by what he's done. Can't admit it to us, or to his parents, maybe not even to himself. So he leaves the body near his father's house. Maybe throwing a little blame in his father's direction at the same time. Nate's childhood wasn't easy."

"None of that sounds far-fetched to me," Bob said.

We drank our coffee.

"Then there's Jody's Toyota being found in Holbrook," Bob said. "Assuming it wasn't stolen by somebody else entirely, and left there— which seems unlikely—Nate may have left it there in order to misdirect us to this person Jody knows in Holbrook. Even if Nate didn't know him by name, he knew of him, am I right?"

"Yes. And he mentioned knowing about him early in the investigation," I said.

"Or maybe Nate just wants to throw us off, complicate our investigation. That covers all the bases—the need to be caught, combined with the desire not to be. He's a contradiction, like everybody else in the world. Did you ever find anybody to verify whether Nate's pickup was in Winslow all night?"

I shook my head. "It was parked in front of an empty house, it turned out. At the houses nearby, and there aren't many, nobody recalled noticing. One person said they remembered a red pickup parked there at midnight; somebody else got the color right but the make wrong, said they saw the vehicle in the morning but weren't sure it had been there the night before."

"The usual witness accuracy, in other words."

"Correct."

"That phone call to Mike Early from the pay phone in Holbrook," Bob said. "You never got any reasonable explanation for that, am I right?"

"Right."

"So Nate calls Mike Early at seven thirty in the morning, in Snowflake," Bob said, "which he knows is reasonably close by, asking for a ride to Winslow. Maybe Nate tells Mike the truth about what he's done, or some version of the truth, and says, 'It's your fault, Mike. I saw you two at the overlook.' Then Nate and Early come up with that alibi about the water leak."

"Or Nate could have made up a story as to why he was in Holbrook," I said. "Then, after Jody's body is found, Mike is implicated. He gave Nate that ride. And he has his own history with Jody. So he keeps quiet. He doesn't know for sure anyway."

"And there's no indication that Kevin Rainey and Mike Early knew each other?"

"None that I could find," I said.

Bob picked up his glasses and turned them around in his hand as he thought.

"We have a lot of circumstantial evidence on Kevin Rainey as well," he said. "Plus he has an assault on his record, plus he has a motive, maybe not as strong as Nate's, but strong enough. Jody doesn't want to see him anymore, won't so much as be friends, and so on. No apologies. Just it's over. I've moved on. Then there are Kevin's parents getting together, after Jody's body is found, deciding to protect him from us, right from the beginning. They suspect him, basically, before we do."

"That's how it seems to me," I said.

"Kevin Rainey also knew quite a bit about Nate, presumably. He would have known about Nate's ties to Black Canyon City."

"Jody was generous with personal details. That's according to a number of people."

"You said that you could see the place where Jody's Toyota was found from Kevin Rainey's trailer?"

"From his living room window."

"Why would he have positioned the body, do you think?"

"I don't know. Control, maybe," I said. "He has none. As you say, she tells him it's over. She won't accept a drink from him. She won't stop telling him about Nate. So Kevin loses his temper and she ends up dead. And once she is, he positions her the way he wants to think of her. A throwaway. She didn't want him; now he doesn't want her. She's under his control now. And maybe he wants to make it look as if Nate

Aspenall has dumped her, literally and figuratively. Give Jody what's coming to her."

Bob was quiet a minute, thinking. "What about Mike Early? Anything else we should be looking at with him?"

"He had more of a relationship with Jody than he wanted us to know. Paying her for sex, basically. Is it possible she didn't want to, with him, that last time? Didn't want to continue the arrangement? Or threatened to tell the ex-wife he wanted to get back together with? But he does have that alibi—not airtight, but the brother-in-law was forthcoming about Early receiving that phone call. My sense was that he was telling the truth, which means Mike couldn't have done it, despite whatever his involvement was afterward."

Bob put on his glasses and looked through the paperwork one more time, while I went to the window. His office was on the third floor, with a view of the courthouse and the downtown streets. The clouds over the hills were lifting and the sun was out. The flag in front of the courthouse was flying briskly.

"Here's the problem we're faced with," Bob said. "The Brady rule. What the prosecution knows, the defense has access to. So if we prosecute Nate, Nate's attorney raises the possibility of Kevin Rainey as the perpetrator, and if we prosecute Kevin, Kevin's attorney raises the possibility of Nate Aspenall. If the Brady rule didn't exist, we might be able to prosecute them one right after the other. It's possible. It would be unusual, but not illegal. But the Brady rule does exist."

"So what do we do?" I said.

"What are the chances of more evidence turning up?"

"As far as physical evidence goes, it's hard to say," I said. "Unlikely but not out of the question. I could imagine Kevin Rainey being foolish enough to talk, but even then it's just hearsay, unless he tells somebody something that might help us, that leads us to evidence perhaps."

"And Nate?"

"Nate is smart and closemouthed. But Mike Early is a different matter. And at present, anyway, he and Nate are neighbors. It's possible that something might happen in the future to make him think twice and give us what we need."

"Any chance of either Nate or Kevin confessing at some point?"

"I don't know," I said. "You know how that goes—time moves on, and people start justifying themselves and their actions that much more. I won't be waiting for it to happen."

We sat in silence, hearing somebody walking past in the hall, and a telephone ringing.

"Frustrating," Bob said.

"Yes."

"So for now," he said, "we arrest nobody and see what happens. As for the family we had hoped to give good news to—well, I guess there isn't much of one."

"No," I said. "We probably care more than Jody's mother will."

chapter forty-six

NATE ASPENALL

E VENING WAS BEGINNING as I drove into Winslow. I lost sight of Jody's car on the interstate between Highway 87 and the Winslow exit, but I caught up with it on Powell Street as she drove east past the high school and the city park to Nelson, where her mother lived. Her mother's trailer was small and white, with a broken step. Parked in front was a red pickup with the passenger door smashed in. Jody parked behind it and went inside without knocking. I heard arguing begin. One voice was male, and it predominated. Then Jody's mother started, and after a few minutes Jody raised her voice, speaking quickly. A woman in the trailer next door came out, listened, then went back in. The arguing continued. I was not close enough to make out the words.

The door flung open, and Jody stood sideways in the doorway, talking loudly. Behind her was the man, small and thin and shirtless. I don't believe he pushed her, but she stepped out stumbling on the broken step and somehow kept herself from falling. She looked at the trailer as if wondering if she should go back in, and she put a hand to her face and pushed her hair back. Then she got in her car, slammed the door, and accelerated fast, heading west toward the high school, then south toward Third Street. I followed a block behind and saw her run a four-way stop. An SUV came close to hitting her. On Third Street she turned into the parking lot of PT's and parked crookedly, and I parked along the street, behind a Suburban. I was close but not so that she could see me. She was reaching for something on the seat beside her or in the glove compartment. Cigarettes, it turned out—one more thing I had not known about her.

It was a clear night with a moon that was still faint. The streetlights had come on. Jody had her window open, and I could see the cigarette smoke drifting out. Except for the movement of her hand she was still. It seemed to me that her hand was shaking. Her car was running and "Pretty Woman" was playing. A long-haired man in overalls appeared without my having seen from where. He went up to her window, and I heard bits and pieces.

" . . . but I live . . . not far. Come . . . we can . . ."

"Don't . . . make . . . asshole . . . Johnny. No."

He had one hand on the roof of her car, and when he persisted she opened her car door and ducked under his arm. Then she half ran, half walked to the bar. He took two steps in her direction, turned, and walked drunkenly down the sidewalk. I wasn't sure how long to wait. *Sometimes I just have a drink or two, Nate, then I go home, where I can be alone, but feeling good.* Men bought her drinks, and she liked the attention, and she was lonely; there was that, too. She would admit those things herself. To an extent she was an honest person. She felt compelled to tell the truth, even as she was tweaking it for her own purposes.

I went just far enough into the bar to see her standing at the other end of it with a drink in her hand, talking to a light-haired man about my age, who wore a blue work shirt. She still wore the ring, despite how crucial it had seemed to her to get rid of it. I wanted her to tell me she wouldn't have married me even if we hadn't seen each other at the overlook, even if I not stayed in Flagstaff, even if I had done as she asked and gone home to Chino Valley and waited for her decision. I wanted her to say that I hadn't come that close. It wasn't the no I couldn't live with. It was the only-if-you-hadn't, the almost-but, the why-would-you-screw-things-up-like-this.

The light-haired man worked out, you could see. A girl walked past and gave him a look. He probably had a regular job and an apartment as opposed to an RV. He and Jody seemed to know each other, although she could behave that way with a man she had met five minutes ago. She had probably eaten nothing since lunch and was drinking on an empty stomach. Then I thought about her and Mike Early at the overlook and the vulgar jokes you could make. What had I been doing asking a girl like that to marry me? Yet if she had walked over and said, *I'm sorry, Nate. Can we still. . .* I would have said yes. But it wasn't in her nature. The tragedy was not what people wouldn't do, I thought, but what they couldn't do.

I ordered a drink and stood near the door; each time it opened I was hidden behind it. The bar was crowded, more so as time passed. The jukebox was playing "Bad to the Bone," and three people in back were arguing over a pool game. Jody moved away from the light-haired man, and a younger man, dark in complexion, reached for her hand and moved her into the space where people were dancing. She held her drink the whole time. She put her hand on his shoulder and danced close to him although that didn't fit the song. He put his mouth to her ear and she laughed, then stepped away and sat alone at a table, tilting back the glass, getting it all down. She looked up suddenly and might have seen me. It was hard to tell. The dark-complected man came between us as he put a drink in front of her. She looked at it as if confused. Then she smiled and picked it up and put her finger in it, touching the ice.

I left before she could see me, held my drink low under my arm, crossed the street and stood behind my pickup and drank and waited. A block away I could see La Posada, the windows lit in the darkness, the well-kept grounds, the bar in which we had sat and talked. I could see the blouse she had worn and the shine of her hair. It was just yesterday, I kept thinking; it seemed so long ago. A hundred lifetimes in a moment, a hundred plans, a hundred years. I saw that what people had done to me they had done, and what I had done to myself and others I had done, and I experienced a second of freedom, standing on that Winslow sidewalk with an empty glass in my hand. The stars were coming out, and the wind was blowing. Jody emerged from the bar and stood in the parking lot with the moon above her. She spun around as she looked at it, Jody at seven in a dancing class, in a skirt and ballet shoes. *Not real ones*, she had told me. *Mine were slippers, Nate. I have kept them for Hannah*. She had taken lessons after school in the basement of the public library. *There were eight of us little girls, Nate, and the teacher didn't like me. If it hadn't been for her, I could have been in the recital.*

The door to the bar opened and the light-haired man stood watching her. We were both watching her. From down the block a man shouted something, then a police car sped past, and the drunken man from earlier was wandering in the street, holding something in his hand. A train was coming. The night was full of sound and motion, as if the future were already here. As if what was going to happen already had.

chapter forty-seven

TRAVIS ASPENALL

"LET TRAVIS STAY," my father said, and I sat at the kitchen table with him, Sam, and my mother. It was almost eight. My mother had made coffee and set out slices of cake. The dogs, who had come in when Sam had, lay close to us as if they knew this was important, that this was what we had been waiting for.

"How's this one settling in?" Sam said, and reached down to scratch the boxer's head. Sam was wearing his uniform. It seemed as if we would never see him as he used to look.

"So?" Dad said.

"I met with the county attorney this morning. We had a long meeting, and you wouldn't want me to go into all the details, believe me. We'd be up until midnight." He smiled thanks to my mother, who was pouring him coffee.

"What can you tell us?" Dad said.

"To start with, there are people besides Nate we've been looking at. I believe I've told you that, Lee, or implied it. In any case we have a good deal of circumstantial evidence, which wouldn't be so problematic

if we weren't looking at more than one person. So we have complica-
tions. That's not unusual. Unless you have somebody caught in the act,
or a clear confession, nothing about a case is simple, and that's true
here. It's doubly true. As a result the investigation is now at a standstill
when it comes to the legalities of the justice system."

"Which means what?"

"Without more evidence we can't prosecute. We can't move forward, on anybody, with what we have."

"What do you mean, more evidence?" Dad said. "What kind of
evidence do you expect at this point?"

"I'm not sure I'd use the word *expect*. But it could happen. Things
cool down, and somebody comes forward, somebody who knows
something or has something or comes across something. Even a confession is possible, although in my experience few people feel that guilty."

"So what you're saying is—" Mom started to say.

"He doesn't know, Julie," Dad said. "There's no certainty about
anything. For all we know a stranger killed Jody Farnell."

"It's not that open-ended," Sam said. "We have a fair amount . . .
well, no point in going into it. I can't anyway."

"But it's possible that somebody you didn't know about," Dad
said, "or couldn't have known about, did this thing."

"That word, *possible*," Sam said, "is tricky. But yes. I suppose so."

The kitchen door was open. Soon it would be summer, I thought,
and this would be in the past, all that had gone on and was going on
now. With every day we woke up to, this would be further away, and
we would be closer to a time when we wouldn't talk about it anymore
and maybe we wouldn't think about it. I kept thinking that the whole
time they were talking.

"But what you're bringing up, Sam, is just evidence and legalities," Mom said. "What do you think happened?"

"Julie," Dad said.

"Listen," Sam said. "It doesn't matter what I think. In fact, I don't much think. I collect information and see what picture emerges. You believe one thing one day and another thing the next. You say something somebody else takes on faith, and it turns out to be wrong. That's the biggest danger."

"The problem with the question is that it's irrelevant," Dad said.

"You could put it that way," Sam said.

"But how would you put it?" Mom asked him.

"The way I just did, Julie."

"We just get on with our lives, finally, and leave it behind us," Dad said.

"Yes," Sam said, "to the extent that you can."

"Meaning everything will be different," Mom said.

"Meaning I don't know what," Sam said. "Honestly."

He looked at the piece of cake on his plate and broke off a piece but didn't eat it.

"What does Nate get told?" Dad said. "Unless or until there's more evidence, et cetera?"

"No. If he asks, I'll say the least I can."

Sam looked at me as if to make sure I understood. Then he rose to leave. Mom wrapped up slices of cake for him, and Dad walked him outside.

THE RING WAS wrapped in a Kleenex shoved into my cowboy boot at the back of my closet. Every night since finding it I had lain awake going through my choices: I could give it to Sam Rush and ask him not to tell Nate where he had gotten it. But I knew that Sam would have to tell the truth in court, if things went that far. I could give the ring to my father and leave it up to him to make the decision and ask him to leave me out of it, which probably he would do. Or I could call Nate saying I needed to tell him something important, and he could leave a message for me on Billy's cell; Nate knew I didn't have one. Or I could put the ring back in the Airstream and leave it for somebody else to find.

Each time I went through the choices I believed there had to be more that weren't occurring to me and that I needed to wait for those to appear. But they never did. I didn't know what the ring meant, but now, after what Sam had told us, it seemed he was waiting for it or something like it.

I locked the bedroom door, got out the ring, put it in the pocket of the jeans I would wear in the morning, folded the jeans, and placed them under the bed. Then I sat and thought, while in the background I heard my parents in their room talking quietly, arguing, then going silent and starting again.

I called Billy and asked if he wanted to go to the Indian Ruins in New River tomorrow. "Can your mom drive?" I said. "That way we can bring your dad's stuff with us. Otherwise we'll have to take Damien."

Once that was arranged I knocked on my parents' door and told them our plans, and they said fine, as long as I was home by six. Then I went back into the bedroom and sat on the bed, listening to the sounds outside and to the television in the den. It wasn't on for long. Mom went in, then Damien came into the bedroom with the dogs coming in after him. After that everything was quiet, including my parents in their universe on the other side of the wall.

BILLY'S MOTHER PICKED us up from school, looking heavier around the middle than she used to, although if I hadn't known, I wouldn't have noticed. She said she would be back at five thirty. "Don't make me wait," she said. "I'll worry." She had gotten us provisions, as she called them, which we put in Billy's backpack; that was where the pot was stashed. I left my backpack in the car.

Then we were on our own, hiking down into and out of the shooting range, then across the stretch of open grazing. The sun was hot and fifty yards or so from us a bull was grazing.

"Want to go fuck with it?" Billy said.

"You go. I'll watch."

"Yeah. Me, too."

As we walked we talked about what we would do that summer. I would work for my dad at the vet clinic four days a week, and Billy would work at the grocery store for Cy the asshole. That was how Billy referred to him, and it was catching. I had come close to saying it in the car with his mother but managed to stop myself.

We made the steep climb to the ruins, then sat in one of the enclosures and lit up the joint. It wasn't easy in the wind. There was nobody around but us—weekends were when people came. Cumulus clouds were billowing up over the big rock formation at the southern edge of New River. It was called Indian Head or used to be. There was a new name nobody could remember. We inhaled the pot as deeply as we could and held it as long as we could, coughing as if we were acting out a Cheech and Chong movie; we used to watch them with Billy's father.

"I don't know where we'll get pot now," Billy said. "I thought about calling Dad's girlfriend, but I hardly know her. Who knows what she might do."

"Just ask at school," I said. "Somebody will know."

"I'll have to get used to that."

"Well, it's not like your dad was giving it to you."

"He knew I helped myself to it," Billy said. "So he got extra. That was how it worked with us."

He lay back on the rocky ground with his backpack under his head, while I looked south over New River, then west at the interstate, where cars and trucks were going somewhere to do something that seemed a thousand miles away from being important.

"I don't suppose your folks would let me live in the Airstream," Billy said.

"They might, but your mom wouldn't."

"When's Nate coming back?"

"No idea," I said.

Billy closed his eyes, and I got up and walked north through one rock enclosure after another until there weren't any anymore, and I was standing at the edge of the steep rock face that led into the mountains. The ring was in my pocket, and I took it out and looked at the coral stone and the silver around it. Decisions you make can affect the rest of your life, my father said, but it was only now that I understood what that meant. Like a lot of things, you had to have it happen first. But even if I had understood beforehand, I'm not sure I would have done anything differently. Because the decision didn't seem to have been made by me. From what I could see, life sometimes told you what to do instead of the other way around. Maybe that was how it was for everybody.

I threw the ring as far as I could and waited to hear the ping of it landing, but the wind was loud, and it was so small. Nobody would ever find it.

acknowledgments

To Jack Shoemaker, Megan Fishmann, Maren Fox, Liz Parker, Kelly Winton, and everybody else at Counterpoint Press, thank you for your exceptional professionalism, artfulness, attention to detail, kindness, and enthusiasm. It was wonderful to work with you.

My heartfelt thanks to Georges and Anne Borchardt for their expertise and unfailing belief in me. I owe them more than I can say.

A thank you to the Yavapai County deputy sheriffs, Dennis McGrane of the Yavapai County Attorneys' Office, Alabama State Trooper David Jones, and Len Williamson for their invaluable help. Any mistakes in the novel are due only to me.

My continued thanks to the Whiting Foundation. I remain grateful every day. My sincere thanks to Mark Siegert, for all his help and support. And a thank you to La Posada, where parts of this book were written.

Above all, I thank Miller—for his honesty and humor, for his doing more than his share, and for twenty years of married love.